FOREVERMORE

ALSO BY LYNN GALLI

VIRGINIA CLAN

Finally

Blessed Twice

Imagining Reality

Wasted Heart

ASPEN FRIENDS

Life Rewired

Something So Grand

Mending Defects

OTHER ROMANCES

Full Court Pressure

Uncommon Emotions

FOREVERMORE

Lynn Galli

Penikila Press

FOREVERMORE. Copyright © 2014 by Lynn Galli. All rights reserved.

This is a work of fiction. Names, characters, events, and incidents are a product of the author's imagination or are used fictitiously. Any resemblance to actual events, locations, or persons, living or dead, is coincidental. The opinions expressed in this manuscript are solely the opinions of the author and do not represent the opinions of the publisher.

Cover photo © 2014 Wongwean/Shutterstock.com. All rights reserved. Used with permission.

No part of this book may be reproduced, scanned, or distributed in any printed or electronic format without the publisher's permission. For information address Penikila Press at penikilapress@yahoo.com. Criminal copyright infringement, including infringement without monetary gain, is punishable by law. Please purchase only authorized electronic or print editions and do not participate in or encourage electronic piracy. Your support of the author's rights is appreciated.

ISBN: 978-1-935611-25-7

Printed in the United States of America.

SYNOPSIS

For M Desiderius, finding someone to love who loves her back was all she could have asked for in life. After marrying Briony and settling in, she begins to hope for even more. Her secret wish is to provide a home for an orphaned girl like she'd been at the age of nine. She owes it to the woman who took her in to pass along that kind act. With Briony's strength and love, she can finally open her home to a foster child.

All would be perfect if not for the fact that Olivia isn't truly theirs. When something happens to put M's dream in jeopardy, will Briony and M find a way to move forward or will the devastating turn punch a hole in their life together that may never be filled?

1

Olivia The elevator ride lasted a whole year. Seasons passed every time another floor went by. I bounced in place, excitement vibrating through me. Two floors to go before my first official job, but I felt like I was aging as we went up and up and up. I'd probably be a teenager by the time we finally got off this thing.

"You have the cellphone, right?" M smiled down at me, her brown eyes glinting in the elevator lights. She liked checking and double checking things. No one had ever been like that with me. Her stepson, Caleb, rolls his eyes about it, but I liked that she was always making sure things were right.

"Yeah." I tapped my coat pocket and felt the slight bulge of her phone.

"Do you have money if you get snacky?" She'd already given me five dollars for the vending machines. She knew she'd already given me the money, but she seemed nervous for some reason.

"Yeah." I couldn't figure out her mood. This wasn't the first time she'd brought me to her friend's office, but she was biting her lip and asking me the same questions she'd already asked on the car ride over from school. "I'll be fine, M."

Her hand came up to adjust the drape of my hair. She'd trimmed it last night to fall two inches past my shoulders. I almost asked her to cut it short like hers, but my round face and plain light brown hair wouldn't look as good short as M's triangular face and rich red-gold highlighted brown hair did. Plus long hair was easier to hide behind. She eyed the ends like she was checking that it was an even cut, but she probably just wanted something to do to keep her mind off whatever was bothering her. When our eyes met, she smiled again. I liked when she smiled. She made everyone feel good when she smiled.

The elevator doors opened—finally. We stepped into a surprisingly cluttered reception area. Normally the game stations were spread out on two walls and the guest chairs spaced around a coffee table in the middle of the area. Today, everything had been pushed aside to make room for two long tables being set up. I didn't have time to wonder if we'd be working out here before the receptionist waved us through as she always did whenever M visited Willa.

Noise blared from every direction once we hit the hallway. Willa's office was always noisy, but today seemed much louder. Up ahead, two guys raced out of a doorway shooting at each other with Ping-Pong guns. M pulled up, putting her arm out and stepping in front of me in case they came our way.

"I swear I will pull this whole office over if you idiots don't stop screwing around!" Willa's voice shouted from inside her office.

I stiffened at the angry tone. Some of my excitement deflated. Willa didn't get angry, even when her friends annoyed her on purpose. I glanced up at M thinking she'd be about ready to turn us around to leave because she was overprotective like that. Instead she was grinning.

It didn't take long to figure out what had made Willa so mad. She was sitting in a cocoon of silly string with Ping-Pong balls cluttering her desk. M burst out laughing. I was more surprised that M was laughing at her friend than I was at seeing Willa trying to get out of the tangle of silly string.

"Nice. Laugh at my misfortune," Willa grumbled. "Olivia, be my best friend and help me out of this mess, will you?"

I rushed over and started pulling away the webbing from her arms and back. I couldn't believe anyone could get away with silly stringing their boss and still keep the job, but Willa's office was weird.

"I take it the Redmond crew is here this week?" M asked her friend.

"Most of them," Willa confirmed, finally free of the string. She stood and started collecting the Ping-Pong balls into her top drawer. "The unfortunate part of finishing up a new game is that everyone has to be together for a few weeks. My people are ready to revolt."

"It is usually more civilized around here," M commented then turned worried eyes toward Willa. "Are you sure the kids are going to be—"

"I'm sure. Really," Willa somehow knew what she meant even when M didn't finish what she was saying. I wish I had a friend like that, but it probably wouldn't happen until I was a grownup. It must take a lot of practice to be a friend like that.

"Where is everyone sitting?" M tilted her head back to glance down the hallway to the main cubicle area.

They kept talking about stuff I didn't quite follow. I knew it wouldn't last long. Unlike most adults, M never did that when kids were around. I tuned out, antsy to get started. For the next two and a half weeks, I'd get to test Willa's newest video game for glitches before it went on sale. She shocked me when she asked if Caleb and I would be interested. I couldn't see how kids would know better than her employees, but she said it was her first kids' game and needed kids' help. She's really smart, so I guess she knows what she's talking about.

"You ready?" Willa gave me an expectant look.

I nodded, happy to get to work. She was paying us a lot to do this. M and Briony objected to the amount at first, but they worked out a deal where half the money would go into a college fund and the rest would go into a savings account as long as we had a savings goal. Caleb and his buddy Hank were saving for new bikes. I made up something but knew I'd only use the money when they kicked me out of their house. Money makes life a lot easier in the group foster homes. Find the alpha girl, pay her, and avoid being bruised "accidentally" when you're five inches shorter than the next shortest girl there.

"Want to stick around, M?" Willa asked.

M's eyes shot to me. She wanted to say yes, but she had another class to teach at college later. My school let out early today. Caleb's middle school wouldn't get out for another two hours. M was probably worried I'd get lost in the activity around here without Caleb looking out for me.

"I've still got one more class."

Willa's lips twitched. She knew what M was thinking. "We'll be here working our fingers to the bone, right, Liv?" She usually called me Liv. Almost everyone else that M and Briony knew called me Livy. Not my favorite, but I didn't want to be rude to their friends. "See?" Willa looked at M after I nodded. "We've got it handled. You head back to campus. I'll drop the kids off around six tonight."

"Sounds good," M said then turned to me. "Have a good time, but pay attention to whoever Willa assigns as your boss."

"I will." I assured her and got an arm squeeze in return before she waved and headed out.

"I think she's afraid one of these idiots might kill you with a Ping-Pong bullet." Willa winked at me.

"Probably." I smiled at her joke, but it felt pretty good to have someone worry about me. Some of my other foster parents didn't realize I was living with them most days. They were overworked, had too many kids, and I was the quiet one. They'd never worry if I was having fun or was completely safe or well fed or had a way to get in touch with them if I needed to. M and Briony were so much like real parents I could forget sometimes that they weren't mine.

"Let's get you set up." Willa gestured toward the door to get us moving. "A couple other kids should be here pretty soon."

I swallowed, trying to keep her from seeing that I wasn't looking forward to any other kids but Caleb and Hank being here. It didn't really matter which kids would be coming. I didn't make friends easily, but I needed this money.

"Olivia, meet Kevin," Willa introduced me to a guy who was setting up the monitors on the tables.

"Hey, Olivia, we're glad to have your help," he said. "You're early, too, we like that, don't we, Will?"

"Sure do. She's going to be your star. Treat her right." She turned to me. "All set?"

I nodded and took a seat. Kevin came over to stand behind me and reached forward to grab a controller and get the game loaded. I tilted to the side to give him more room and make sure he knew that I knew he was there—lesson number one for a foster kid.

"These are the main controls here." He pressed against the two thumbsticks on each side of the controller. "Are you good at video games?"

Until I got to use Caleb's, I'd never really played video games before. My mom didn't have the money and no foster parent had a gaming console. "I'm not really sure."

He leaned down. "You're not a gamer?"

He looked concerned. Maybe I should lie. I needed this money, but I shouldn't lie. Not if it would hurt Willa's company. "No, sir."

"Kevin," he insisted as a wide grin came over his face. "You'll be perfect for this. We never get beginners testing games. Willa!"

Willa appeared a few seconds later. "You bellowed?"

"Whose kid is this doll?" His thumb hooked toward me, and I felt my stomach clench. "You need to give them a raise for finding us a virgin gamer."

"Kev!" Willa scolded. Her tone made me jump in my seat. Uh-oh, he was in trouble. "Vocabulary."

"Oh, shh—um, shoot, right. Yeah, okay, can do. Sorry, Olivia, I wasn't thinking."

I wish they'd stop talking and just let me get to work. They didn't need to worry about me. He could say whatever he wanted. I'd heard a lot worse in the homes I'd lived in. M and Briony's was the first house that had a no-swearing rule. It was easy for me, but Briony sometimes let a word slip. She had to pay a dollar into the swear jar when she did. Caleb said we'd get to go to Six Flags when it had enough money in it.

"Whose kid is she?" he asked Willa.

I wanted to crawl under the desk. I hated this question. I didn't like talking about not having a mom anymore. Why couldn't people understand that?

Before Willa answered, the elevator dinged and two of the meanest girls in my class stepped off. Now I really wanted to disappear. Of all the girls in school to be here, it had to be these two. My heart sank, taking most of my excitement down with it.

2

Olivia "Hey, Willa," Krystal beamed at her.
"Yeah, like, hi," Kortney tried to match Krystal's enthusiasm.
"Hi, ladies," Willa greeted them. "We're just getting started. Do you know Olivia?"

Both girls turned to look at me. Kortney sighed but Krystal groaned until she saw that Willa was watching her. "Yeah, sure, she's in our class."

Willa squinted at her for a second. "Good, then you should all have fun today. Why don't you head back and say hi to your dads." She watched them go before turning back to me. "Are you all friends?"

No. But I didn't say that. Adults didn't like to hear that kids weren't friends with everyone in their class. It made them think something was wrong with you. "Um," I started.

"Let me put it this way," Willa cut in as her dark eyes drilled into mine. "Do you have a problem working with them?"

"No," I blurted. I wouldn't have a problem, but they might.

"Because if you do, I can ask them to leave."

She'd ask them to leave? Even though they had dads who worked here and I didn't? "No, it's okay."

She stared at me for a bit longer. She was like M that way. They could both read expressions. "All right then. Kev, get Olivia started and work with the girls when they get back. Caleb and some friends plus Mike's son will be here in a couple hours."

Kevin came back over and told me to open up a blank document for notes on the things I found wrong. I started the game and went to the help menu to learn how to play it. That was when the other girls came back. Kevin gave them the same instructions then let them start. He watched us for a while before he came over to help me with all the different controls.

The girls giggled from the other end of the room. I knew they were laughing about me, but I didn't care. I couldn't let it bother me. Girls had been laughing at me since my mom died, about my clothes, about the houses I lived in, about my grades, about a lot of things. I used to get really upset, but it never helped anything.

Two hours later, I was still working through the first level while the other girls had made it to level four. It sucked that they were ahead of me, but it took me a long time to read through the instructions, menus, and screens. I wasn't so good at reading.

When Kevin left us to make a call in his office, Krystal said, "He's cute."

"Supe cute," Kortney said back. She never had an original thought. She always just agreed with Krystal.

"Don't know why he's wasting time on the freak," Krystal went on.

I thought they'd forgotten about me. Hoped they had. I hated when they did this. They picked on so many kids in our class, but I was their favorite because I never talked back. I tried to ignore them, but sometimes it made them pick on me more.

"She's stupid, that's why," Kortney told her.

"She's a retard, more like," Krystal said.

I flinched. That word, I hated it. Mom always told me not to hate things, but I'd heard that word used around me before. Last year, they tried to hold me back at school. It was the reason my last set of foster parents sent me back to the group home. If I'd stayed in that school district, I probably would have been held back. That was one nice thing about jumping foster homes. A new district meant new records and teachers and time to convince everyone I wasn't dumb. Briony and M didn't think I was. They helped me with homework, explained things so I could understand them, and treated me like I was as smart as everyone else in my class, even if I wasn't. Whenever I got frustrated, M tried to convince me that smart had a lot of sides to it. Sometimes I believed her, but it was hard when Krystal and her flock started making fun.

"Supe retard," Kortney agreed.

"Yeah, like, 'member when Mrs. Lomax asked her to read out loud last week? It took her, like, all day to read one paragraph."

"Forevs," Kortney said.

I could feel tears starting and that embarrassed me more. I wasn't good at reading out loud either. Even worse than when I read to myself. M helped me practice, but I'd probably never be good at it. I didn't feel stupid, but Krystal and her friends could change my mind about that.

"Do you need help reading the game, freak?" Krystal called out. "Do you even know the whole alphabet?"

I looked over to the receptionist. Thankfully she was on the phone. I didn't want her to hear what they were saying.

"Are you deaf and a retard?" Krystal asked.

I continued to ignore them. Saying anything would only make them continue. Their attention spans were shorter than their miniskirts. They usually moved on quickly.

Willa came into the reception area. "How's it going, ladies?"

They made a big show of saying how much they loved it and couldn't believe they were getting paid. I took the opportunity to escape to the bathroom while they were falling all over Willa. It was nice to get away from their constant chatter.

A few minutes later, I headed back to my workspace. Willa was talking to the girls out in reception. "Really? Because I think calling someone a freak and a retard is cruel and offensive."

I stopped in the hallway. I didn't want to eavesdrop, but as a foster kid, it was how I kept from being surprised all the time.

"We were kidding around, Willa, come on," Krystal said.

"You might be able to fool your parents with your innocent act, but I know if I called you those things, you wouldn't think I was kidding. Your feelings would be hurt."

"She can't even read!" Krystal protested. "She's, like, super dumb."

"That's it," Willa said in a chilling voice. "I'm not going to treat either of you like you're too young to know the difference. I know you understand that what you said was hurtful, and still you said it. That's not just a mean thing to say. It's a mean thing to do. I don't like mean girls."

"We're not mean," Kortney screeched. "We're the most popular girls in school."

"Popularity has nothing to do with being nice. You guys are done here."

"No, we're not," Krystal talked back. "We're only on level four, and it's the first day."

"I don't hire mean girls," Willa told them.

"Yeah, but, but," Kortney stuttered.

"Come on, Kort. Dad will do something about this," Krystal said in that annoying know-it-all voice she had. "I thought you were cool, Willa."

"Krystal, look at me," Willa paused and waited for Krystal to follow her order. "Your dad works for me. I pay his salary. If you want to whine to him about this, he's going to hear what I have to say and he'll believe me. If you don't want that to happen, head on back and tell him you're bored and don't want to do this anymore."

"Whatevs!" Krystal said.

I backtracked to the bathroom, sick to my stomach that Willa had to hear that the girls in my class thought I was dumb. I didn't want her to have to deal with them. Maybe I could get their jobs back. It was going to be awful going back out there. Willa was going to lie to make me believe that they left on their own. Adults usually tried to soften things for kids.

The bathroom door opened to show Willa's face. "Liv, come to my office for a sec."

I followed her back to her office and heard the girls pass behind us with their dads. At least I wouldn't be in the reception area when they left. It sounded like they were giving them the "bored" story. I didn't blame them.

I'd barf up my lunch if Briony or M heard something bad about me from Willa.

Willa tried to look happy, but I could tell she wasn't. Like the time her friend Des kept asking me about my mom in front of all of their friends. That was so embarrassing. M got me out of there, but not before I saw Willa's face go red and her eyes glare at Des.

I waited for her lie. I guess I should be thankful that there were adults in my life that would think a lie would be better than the truth if it hurt, but I didn't like lies.

"If someone is purposefully mean to you, you can call them on it, you know?"

I looked up from my lap. She wasn't sugarcoating it for me?

"I try not to sink to their level, but I call them on it." She looked at me, but I didn't know what to say. "I guess that might not always work with kids, though, right?" She waited for my nod. "And I might have just made things worse for you at school, too, huh?"

I couldn't nod at that one. She meant well, but she just made sure I'd be cornered at school tomorrow. It was pretty cool that Willa took my side, though.

"Well, crap." Willa sat back, thinking.

"It's fine," I tried to reassure her.

"It's not, but I couldn't let those little brats stay here. Krystal's been driving me nuts for two years ever since I hired her dad."

I laughed. Adults never spoke this way around me.

"Hey, what's going on in here?" Caleb showed up in the doorway wearing his trademark big smile. "Aren't you supposed to be working?"

"Is someone speaking, Liv?" Willa asked me, not even looking at Caleb. "I distinctly remember saying that I don't talk to thirteen-year-olds who are taller than I am."

I giggled at Willa's comment. They were always kidding each other.

"Aww, Willa, you love talking to me," he replied easily.

"Correction, I used to love talking to you until you outgrew me, punk!"

"I can still hear you from up here," he taunted, coming over to stand next to her. He was barely half an inch taller than Willa at a few inches over five feet. He had big feet, though, so he was probably going to grow a lot more. "Come on, Livy, Hank and Terrence are out front. Show us what you've been doing so we can start earning some bucks."

I never minded when Caleb or Briony called me Livy, just when everyone else did. They let me live with them, so they could call me anything they wanted. Plus they meant it affectionately not like they thought I was still a baby.

I smiled at Willa and headed back out with Caleb. He and Hank were always really nice to me. He didn't seem to mind that I was more than a year younger and a girl. He treated me like a brother would. It made me feel good to be around him. It would take my mind off of having to deal with the mean girls tomorrow.

3

The student stared at me with eyes pleading, but they lacked sincerity. Oh, he wanted his grade changed. That was sincere enough, but his ask didn't have the conviction of someone who understood he'd screwed up and needed a pass. He just wanted me to change his grade without having done anything to fix his case study. He thought by scheduling the appointment and coming in to see me that I would do as he asked. Some professors did that. They didn't like denying the request or didn't want to do the extra work to help the student get a better grade. I wasn't like that.

My eyes shifted to check that my office door was still open. I usually conducted these types of appointments in my classroom, but it was in use and he didn't want to wait. They never wanted to wait when their GPA was on the line. He was graduating at the end of the term, and this paper's C was threatening to bring his current A in the class down to a B+, which didn't sit well with him. I rolled my chair a foot closer to the door. He wasn't crowding me. I set up the chairs in my office specifically to keep students from crowding me, but he was pretty eager about me changing his grade.

"See what I did here?" His finger pointed to an aesthetically pleasing section in the paper. He formatted his papers exactly how I liked them, but he'd dropped the ball on content this time. "I posited that the belt speed kept the line from maximum efficiency. I bet no one else did that, Prof."

Everyone else had done that. It was an operations management class. Factory output was always the first item analyzed. "It isn't enough to state the theory. You need to prove it. You should have noted the actual speed. Then if it was increased by X amount, it would have resulted in an increase in X number of units each day."

"But," he sighed and couldn't come up with another argument, much like his lacking paper.

"You had a project due in another class and slapped this together at the last second because you can write these things in your sleep, right?" I guessed.

He shrugged. It was funny how college age men could become exactly like my teenage stepson when called on their crap.

"It's easy to let things slide in the home stretch, especially when you know a certain subject comes easy to you." I tried not to let my tone slip into lecture mode. "Your conclusions are all correct, but you don't have any analysis or proof to back them up."

"What can I do? I can't let my grade slip in this class, Professor D."

Now we were getting somewhere. The pleading had turned to reason, and his eyes showed his honesty. I always had extra work for anyone wanting to improve their grades. The University of Virginia was hard enough, the graduate business program one of the best. They'd done the hard work getting accepted. The least we as professors could do was help them to achieve the best grades their level of work commanded.

I turned back to my desk and fingered through the shelves until I found the case study I always kept available for extra work. I pulled a copy from the shelf and handed it to him. "By Thursday's class. Do a thorough job this time, and it gets added to your grade count to help minimize the effect of the C on this study."

His shoulders fell a bit, but he bounced back pretty quickly with a cheeky smile. "No chance you can just replace the C with the one I'll get on this paper?"

"No chance." My tone was firm. My students knew they could get away with quite a bit in my class, joking around, talking over each other, talking out of turn, but I wasn't a softie when it came to grades.

"Thanks anyway." He stood and headed for the open door.

I glanced down at my laptop and checked to make sure he was the last appointment of the day. Shutting down the computer, I sorted through my lecture notes until I found the topic for tomorrow's classes. Those were added to my bag with the laptop and I exited, pausing to lock the office.

Several doors stood open in the hallway. My stomach clenched. In the past, I would have walked right over to the staircase without even glancing into the offices much less saying anything to anyone on my way out. These days I had to be seen making an effort for Briony's sake. She was a well-liked faculty member on campus. At first no one understood why she'd be with me, the faculty outcast. Over the last couple of years, she'd gotten me to attend more faculty functions and people were forced to deal with me. They still considered me odd, didn't understand Briony and me together, but no one seemed to fear me as they used to. I would be happy to go back to barely speaking to anyone, but because it would reflect poorly on Briony, I made an effort.

The first two offices had student appointments. The professor in the third was on the phone. Only one more open office door before the staircase. Fourteen steps away. I could do this.

Dr. Goldberg looked up as I was passing by. Tension tightened my neck and shoulders. I'd maybe spoken to this guy once at a faculty party. I knew nothing about global marketing and that was pretty much all he talked about.

"Afternoon." I added what I hoped was a friendly expression and nod of my head.

"Dr. Desiderius," he replied and looked like he wanted to say more, but my pace had taken me past his office and the stairwell door loomed in front of me.

I tried not to take the stairs two at a time as if running from any possible encounter, but it was difficult to break old habits. Meeting someone on the stairwell was even worse than walking past an open office door. Thankfully, it was getting hotter outside and almost everyone took the elevators when it was hot outside.

Pushing through the exit door, I felt the first wave of spring heat roll over me. The end of March shouldn't be this warm, but it was a nice change from the frigid days we'd had in February. I checked my watch and smiled at the time. I could make a detour before I had to pick up the kids.

Briony's class schedule flashed in my mind. She had a venture capital overview class going right now. Was it in the i.Lab or not? No, on Mondays, she was over in the regular classrooms. That gave me just enough time.

As I stepped onto one of the brick pathways crossing Flagler Court, my eyes caught sight of a familiar figure. Quinn, the women's head basketball coach, was striding toward Saunders Hall. I didn't often see her at work. If I did, it would be closer to her office at the sports complex, but occasionally she came up this way for the excellent café.

Any normal human would go over and greet her friend. Quinn was a nice lady, married to the best friend I had. Of course, I should go over and say hello. I shouldn't immediately want to duck back into the faculty building to ensure that she not see me. We could talk. I'd talked to her at many of her dinner parties, but she wasn't Willa. No one in the group was Willa, and because of that, I still wasn't comfortable striding over with the sole purpose of striking up a conversation.

I checked my watch again. If I went to say hello I might miss my window with Briony. If I didn't and Quinn saw me, I'd probably be teased relentlessly at the next dinner. Physical torture would be easier than enduring everyone's attention focused on me.

Sucking in a deep breath, I took one step in her direction. I had to become more comfortable with this. It had been three years that I'd known Briony and by extension these friends of hers. Several years that I'd known Willa and her partner, Quinn. I should be able to do this without breaking out into a sweat or counting just to get through it.

On the fourth step, a group of students approached Quinn and surrounded her. If not for her exceptional basketball caliber height, I would have lost sight of her. Seeing that the group wasn't going to move on quickly, I swiveled back toward Briony's classroom. This was an acceptable diversion. I could feel good about avoiding Quinn today.

A few students greeted me as I walked toward Briony's classroom. I never had any problem greeting students. I stopped trying to analyze why I wasn't a social freak with students but I was with people I'd known for years.

At the door, I stopped and peered through the glass. Her students clumped together in the first two rows of seats. Any other professor would have had to bribe the students not to spread out in the five tier room, but Briony's students clustered around her naturally. Most of her entrepreneurial courses were electives, which meant smaller sizes and specialized interest. Four of mine were in the core curriculum, which meant more students but many would rather be in a different class. I often envied Briony her specialty.

With two minutes left in class, I felt okay about slipping inside. Nearly every head turned when I did. That always bothered me, but because I'd already met with this class, it wasn't unusual for me to be here.

"Hey, Professor D!" one of the students called out, inciting a few similar greetings.

I smiled at them and shifted my eyes to my beautiful partner. Her blond hair had grown out a bit since I'd first met her. The long layered cut suited her as well as the shorter version I'd fallen for. After three years together, I knew every inch of her trim body, how it felt against me, in my hands, under my mouth. It looked just as good wrapped in her elegant professional dress as it did naked in our bedroom.

"Nice of you to join us, Professor," Briony's voice spilled over me, soothing every frayed nerve I experienced from the walk over here. "I was just telling the class that you'll be part of the pitch deck evaluations."

My eyebrows rose. It made sense to have me there, but we hadn't talked about it first. Usually she accommodated my more reticent attitude toward new activities, but she must have orders from the dean on this one.

"I'm sure they'll be dazzling," I spoke to the class, basically telling them they had better dazzle us if they wanted to be one of the two businesses to get funding through our summer venture class.

The bell rang and most of the students raced for the door. Three went up to Briony but wouldn't stay long. Time was short so Briony would move them along. I headed toward her. This sometimes hastened the departure of students. Today was no disappointment. Within a few minutes, the last of the students slipped out the classroom door.

"Hello there, sexy prof." Her tone no longer held any trace of the reserved professionalism that greeted me when I walked in the door. Her eyes raked over me, seeming to enjoy every bit of the view. The heat I encountered outside didn't come close to what one of these perusals could do to me. "What brings you over?"

"You," I answered honestly. Games that might make her insecure or incite jealousy so she'd always be working to find out how much I loved her were pointless, and I'd never be good at them anyway.

She blew out a long breath. "Thanks, I needed that today."

"Hard day so far?"

"You might have guessed that Dean Goudy stopped by. He wants these proposals in top notch condition before they're presented. He brought up the three businesses that are no longer operational now."

"Oh, please." University politics were so exasperating. "All three companies were bought out at a huge profit. What do they have to complain about?"

"It feels like they're trying to document failures to justify killing the program."

"Then why not just kill it? It's not like we're dying to teach this class every summer."

"I'll be forever grateful to it because I got to know you." She shrugged and looped her arms around me. "But you're right; I wouldn't miss having to teach every summer."

I glanced over my shoulder to make sure no one was spying on us through the window in the door. We were one of five married couples on the faculty and remained professional in the public spaces. But behind closed doors, we didn't always follow that policy.

Her hand came up to caress my cheek, fingers drawing the line of my jaw. "You off to pick up the kids?"

"Thought I'd just leave 'em there for a few hours," I joked. We traded off dropping off and picking up the kids from school every semester depending on our class schedules. I actually preferred picking up to dropping off. It gave me the excuse to leave campus before dark each day.

"You've got about thirty seconds," she reminded me as her fingers moved down to trace the column of my throat.

I'd be fine just standing here in her arms for the rest of the afternoon, but thirty seconds would do nicely. "Missed you this morning," I said. She'd hustled out the door, running too late to stop back into the bedroom to say our customary goodbye.

"I nearly had to yank Caleb's arms out of his sockets to get him out of bed this morning. I'm starting to think we need to change his bedtime to an hour earlier."

"I think it's more likely that he's not going to sleep at lights out." I'd heard noise from Caleb's room an hour or two later on many nights.

"I might have to clear out his room every night, huh?"

"Take the iPad away at least. Those brainless games are addictive."

"You always have good ideas." Her eyes flashed before she pushed in for a kiss. Her mouth was soft and warm against mine. My stomach did a lazy summersault at the first press of her lips. Even three years later, a simple kiss exhilarated me.

Pulling back, I sighed, resting my forehead against hers. "I better go if I want to beat the bell."

"Wear the kids out this afternoon so we can get them in bed early." Her eyebrows bobbed playfully.

I chuckled and brushed my mouth against hers once more before ending my happy diversion. "See you later, sweetheart."

4

At the elementary school I drove past the mile long line of cars waiting to pick up kids in the loading area and turned into the school's parking lot. I'd tried waiting in the line once but sucking down exhaust fumes as we edged forward one car at a time lost its appeal after one try.

The kids could ride the bus, but the schools were on the way home from campus and one of us needed to be at home for Olivia. Briony and I thought they were old enough to be home alone for a couple of hours after school, but Olivia's social worker wasn't there yet. Next year, possibly.

Olivia came into view, walking alone, like usual. It pained me to see her not talking to the other kids. I knew she ate lunch with some fifth graders, but so far only a couple of kids in her class even acknowledged her let alone spoke to her. She thought I didn't know, but I didn't need to be an anthropologist to recognize the hordes of sixth grade girls as they emerged. She'd wave to a couple of kids from time to time, but no one huddled close and spoke animatedly whenever I came by to pick her up. I just hoped she could hold on until next year when she moved across the street to the middle school and changed classes every hour. She'd have a much better chance of making friends her own age since this wasn't the only elementary school that would feed into the middle school. And with outgoing Caleb around, he'd introduce her to everyone he knew.

She gave me a wide smile when she spotted me. I lived for that smile. Back in October when she first came to live with us, she barely spoke more than a few words voluntarily. Incredibly shy, she seemed to be waiting for us to just dump her back into the system. As Caleb drew her out, one of his best qualities, he helped make her feel more secure in our home life and now she smiled and talked freely. She'd probably never be a motor mouth, but she didn't wait until someone asked her a question before she spoke anymore.

"Hi, Olivia. Did you have a good day?"

"Yep," she said, like she always did. She could get upset when she couldn't figure out her homework because she thought she wasn't smart enough, but she never seemed to get upset that she didn't have friends coming over to play or a best friend to share her secrets with.

We took a seat on the low wall that sectioned off the landscaping from the sidewalk. Her feet dangled a few inches from the ground. Just a slip of a girl, she might not get much taller than me at five-two. Sunlit brown hair whipped across her face until she turned her head into the breeze. Stick straight, her hair dropped to her shoulder blades in one length. She looked cute as hell the way she was now, but she didn't like that the tops of her ears pushed against the fine strands. Whenever someone outside the family focused on her, she'd self-consciously tucked it behind her ears. The sprinkle of freckles across her slightly protracted nose and big, milk chocolate eyes told me she'd grow into her looks.

Thankfully, she wasn't one of those girls who seemed concerned about that.

"How's your homework load?"

"Just math and science tonight." She smiled because she liked math and science. Language arts, what used to be called English in my day, was her least favorite.

"Will you have enough time after dinner?" I'd been a little worried that work might cut into homework time every night. She took longer than Caleb to finish. If she came to us for help sooner, she'd get it done more quickly, but we admired that she tried to tackle everything on her own. Depending on the subject, Caleb might just give it a glance before heading right to us for help.

"Yep. I did half my math worksheet when Mrs. Lomax got called to the office after lunch."

I nodded and looked up as I heard the middle school kids swarm out of the building across the street. Caleb, Hank, and Terrance would be here in a few minutes. I was their ride to Willa's. The boys loved it, but it seemed to have lost its luster for Olivia. Caleb was the gamer in the house. She'd only play if he asked her. I could see how testing a new game might not be as appealing to her as it would be for the boys.

"Are you still having fun at Willa's?"

Her head and shoulders bobbed in an enthusiastic display that wasn't entirely genuine. She wouldn't want to hurt Willa's feelings or disappoint anyone by dropping out of a project.

"We could tell her you have too much homework. She won't mind."

She looked away, shrugging but shaking her head. I liked that she followed through on commitments, but I also knew the environment was overwhelming for her.

"Hiya," Caleb called out as he and the boys walked up to us. Due to a recent growth spurt, Caleb now stood two inches taller than Hank, but not yet as tall as Terrance. They were an odd bunch. From what I'd seen, most boys kept their hair the same length. These three bucked that trend. Hank had longish hair that looked like it needed a perpetual cut, Terrance's curls were short but full, and Caleb asked me to keep his blond hair tight on the sides and a touch longer on top. He was the easiest haircut in the house.

"Ready?" Hank signed rather than spoke as he'd been doing more and more lately. Terrance and Olivia were still learning sign language, but they knew enough to keep up. The rest of his friends made the effort to learn a good mix of words, so he wouldn't have to read lips all the time. It made going to a hearing school much easier for him. Now that he had a fluent best friend, friends willing to try, and an interpreter for classes, he didn't feel as isolated as he used to. He'd never be the chatterbox that Caleb was, but he could communicate with almost anyone now.

"Let's split, bananas," Caleb signed and spoke almost as naturally as Hank and I did.

I herded the kids to my car. In all my life, I never thought I'd become a parental unit who needed a minivan to sit four or more kids comfortably. At the dealership, I found I couldn't go through with it and swerved toward the midsized SUVs instead. Coming from a coupe, I was still getting used to this massive people mover.

Willa greeted us as the elevator opened on her floor. "My brilliant testers, perfect timing. Terrance, your mom needs to see you before you start. The rest of you, follow me. You can be my focus group."

We barely made it a few steps inside her now crammed office. Colorful posters, mugs, pens, bags, and boxes were scattered around the room.

"Cool," Caleb said as he took it all in.

"We're trying to decide what to order for game paraphernalia," Willa told us. "Nykos and I can't agree on what we like best. It's up to you guys now."

Olivia glanced around as if worried that Nykos would appear. A big, loud guy, he intimidated me, too. If he weren't so funny and good to Willa, I'd probably try to avoid him.

The boys went to inspect everything closer. Olivia stood by my side, taking it all in from a distance. Everything looked market quality to me, but I knew Willa would only make some of these items available. She wasn't into paraphernalia like her business partner was.

"Rad," Caleb said, holding up a blue and black messenger bag.

"Epic." Hank picked up the bag next to it in green instead of blue.

"Your preference, Liv?" Willa asked, her eyes sliding briefly to mine. She was up to something, and I hoped I was guessing right about it.

"They're both nice," Olivia told her.

"How about this one?" She pulled a black backpack with purple side panels out of the box by her feet.

Olivia's favorite color. Yes, Willa's intent became clear. Olivia's backpack was falling apart. Briony had already sewn three patches into it because Olivia wouldn't let us buy her a new one. She didn't like us buying things for her. She was very money conscious. I suspected she'd been told time and time again just how expensive it was to raise kids by other foster parents. We'd used Christmas as an excuse to get her some much needed new clothes and Caleb's birthday as another excuse to get her a new outfit so she wouldn't feel left out with all the presents he got.

"This one, huh?" Willa guessed when she noticed that Olivia's eyes hadn't left the backpack. "It's about what we thought. We're going to have to produce all three. You guys get the sample editions."

Bless her. I'd mentioned once that Olivia wouldn't let us shop for her, and this wonderful woman figured out a way to get Olivia to take a much needed new backpack. Olivia's eyes grew wide while the boys high fived each other and showed off their bags.

"Liv?" Willa held out the backpack.

"Don't you need them?" Her eyes were still glued to the bag.

"No, these are samples. We pick the best and tell the manufacturer to mass produce them. The ones that come off the line might be a little different, but not by much."

"Don't you want it? Or someone who works here?" Olivia persisted, looking first at Willa then up to me.

"Nope. We all have company logo bags, so these are yours. You'll be my secret gorilla marketers at your school." She tossed Olivia the bag.

I reached a hand out to run over the material. It felt as good as it looked. Olivia zipped it open and went through all the inside pockets. "That'll hold all your stuff, yeah?" She grinned and practically vibrated with excitement. "Briony's going to be jealous she didn't get one."

Her head snapped up and she pushed the bag toward me. "She can have this one."

My hand went to my heart. This kid was too considerate for words. She had something in her hands that she really wanted and she was willing to give it up. "Oh, sweetie, no. I was kidding. This bag's perfect for you." I glanced at Willa, who looked equally impressed with Olivia's offer, and then we both looked away. I could feel tears prick my eyes.

"Yeah, that one's yours," Willa confirmed. "If Briony wants one, I might let her buy one off our site. But only if she's good."

"Thank you so much," Olivia offered in an amazed voice, soliciting the same from the boys.

"Maybe I want a backpack," Caleb joked as he made a move toward her bag.

"Keep your paws to yourself, punk," Willa ordered and grabbed his shoulders, sliding him into a locking hold. Hank giggled as Caleb struggled to break the hold. He was getting a lot stronger, but that hold was pretty effective.

"C'mon, guys," Terrance shouted as he passed by Willa's office on the way out to the lobby workstations.

Willa let Caleb free and he and Hank sprinted after their friend. Olivia lingered, not as eager to get started.

"Is Helen here yet?" I asked of Willa's chef sister, who usually came to town to prepare dinners for Willa's staff right before they launched a game.

"Last night. She's already whining about needing help in the kitchen. I should have checked Quinn's schedule before deciding on a launch date. Normally they cook together."

"You're not going to do it, are you?" I kidded. My friend was a wonderful, generous person, who ran her business better than anyone I'd ever met, but she was a disaster in the kitchen.

"Ha-ha. I'm a pretty good prep chef. Just don't let me cook anything."

"Liv's a great cook," I bragged and Olivia startled next to me before a blush hit her cheeks. She helped in the kitchen all the time and really seemed to like it. I didn't think Willa would mind if I angled for a different job.

"Really? Do you like it, Liv?" Willa asked her.

"Sure," she admitted.

"My sister's in town. She cooks for the crew during crunch time to ensure we get at least one healthy meal a day. She could use the help if you're interested."

Olivia looked at me first, asking permission. She did this for almost everything—yet another habit picked up by living in foster homes. I swallowed hard as memories came flooding back. I'd hated the foster homes I lived in and not just because of what happened to me in one of them. Nothing felt good about living under different rules in every house, tiptoeing around the parents, avoiding the permanent and temporary kids, and never, ever feeling at home. For Olivia, hers weren't nearly as bad, but they had been overpopulated.

"I bet Helen would be grateful for the help," I encouraged her.

"Sous chefs earn five dollars more an hour than testers, Liv," Willa said, making me want to both smack her and thank her. The kids were already making double minimum wage testing the games.

"You'd pay me?" Olivia asked in wonder.

"Of course. Helen's going to work you pretty hard."

"She doesn't mind having a kid around?"

Willa shook her head and smiled. "She digs kids. You guys will get along great. If M has time, let's all go over to meet her and help out a bit. If you like it, the job's yours. If not, you come back with me and continue testing."

Olivia's eyes pinged back to mine. "Do you have time?"

I had papers to grade and had been looking forward to a couple of quiet hours at home, but this was a good opportunity for Olivia. Technically a work situation, she could be left alone with Helen without the need for a background check, but I could hear the social worker's sound of disapproval in my head. I'd call her tomorrow to let her know that Olivia was reporting to a new supervisor. She liked to be consulted first, but she almost always agreed with our suggestions. Since Willa had already gone through a background check in case we needed child care, the social worker probably wouldn't have an issue with Olivia's change in work location. For today, I could chaperone especially since it would give Olivia more confidence with Helen. "Sure. If you don't mind me grading papers while you guys work."

"Okay," Olivia agreed, still somewhat subdued because she didn't like showing her excitement. She'd been let down too many times before coming to live with us. It was the one thing I wish I could change about her, and I hoped to have a lot more time to work on it.

5

Olivia When M and Briony knocked on my bedroom door, I could tell something was wrong. They'd been really happy after Willa dropped me off from my last day cooking with Helen. All throughout dinner, everything seemed fine, but now something was wrong.

Briony sat on the bed facing me at my desk. M placed a hand on her shoulder, standing behind her. This was different from other homes. When one kid got in trouble, whichever parent was home usually started yelling right away. Here, whenever Caleb did something wrong, one of them would tell him to stop and then wait for the other to get home to sit him down and talk it over together. Those talks always started just like this.

"Your teacher called us today," Briony said, and something heavy dropped in my stomach. The teacher calling was never a good thing. "She said you haven't turned in your homework for two days. Is that true?"

Darn. I should have known this teacher wouldn't let it slide. That was the other bad thing about being a foster kid; everyone thinks they need to parent you. If it had been anyone else in my class, she would have given them an incomplete until they turned in the assignments. With me, she calls my foster parents to tell on me.

"I'm sorry. I didn't get it done."

M nodded her head, looking like she wanted to say something, but thinking about it. M always thought before she spoke.

"Why did you tell us you didn't have any homework? We don't lie to each other in this house." Briony didn't sound mad, but I knew she had to be. I lied and was going to get bad grades.

I shook my head, upset at myself. My grades weren't the best and not turning in these assignments wasn't going to help. Briony and M were super smart college professors who taught super smart students. They had to be so disappointed in me.

"Olivia?" Briony tried again, her tone firmer. She wasn't yelling yet, but she wasn't a yeller like some of the other foster parents.

Tears pricked my eyes. I knew what this meant. Bad grades were one thing but lying wasn't allowed. Caleb lost television and gaming privileges for two weeks the last time he lied about telling his mom he asked M for permission to go over to his friend's house. This was a lot bigger deal than that. I wouldn't be losing privileges for something major like this. No, it would be something much worse. I was so stupid. This home was the best thing going here and I went and screwed it up.

Before they told me to do it, I stood and went to my closet. I reached for my duffle bag, feeling my throat go dry as I tried to remember which clothes I'd brought with me and which ones they'd given me.

M was behind me before I heard her. "You're not leaving. This isn't…that's not what we're saying."

"Oh, honey, no," Briony rushed over and grasped my arms. "Never." She pulled me into a tight squeeze.

I loved these hugs. She wasn't the first foster parent to hug me, but Briony was really good at giving them. It wasn't just when she thought she had to. Sometimes she'd just grab me or Caleb as we walked by for a surprise hug. I looked up and saw M watching us with a worried look on her face.

"This is your home, Olivia," M told me. "We won't ever ask you to leave."

I shook my head against Briony's shoulder, eyes feeling heavy and wet. I couldn't believe what they were saying. They couldn't mean they'd never kick me out. The foster mom before my last one told me the same thing. Three months later her husband left her, and she didn't feel like keeping me and the two other foster kids anymore. It didn't matter that I'd felt safer and more secure here than any other place. That I felt like it was the closest thing to living with my mom than any other place I'd lived. Every house kicks me out. I get too expensive or I don't help out enough or the other kids in the house don't like me or the parents didn't want a dummy living in their home. I always get kicked out. Then it's back to the group home where I try to disappear until I get placed in another foster home.

Briony pulled back to look at me but didn't let me out of her arms. "You did make a mistake, kiddo. You lied about not having any homework. Was it too hard? Did you need help?"

"We'll always find time to help," M added.

I swallowed hard. "You said I couldn't cook with Helen if I didn't finish my homework." And I never would have gotten it done in time. Reading takes forever.

"School comes first," Briony insisted.

My shoulders dropped in defeat. I knew that rule, too. I'd broken two house rules in two days. "I didn't want to let Helen down. She had so much to do and she needed help."

Briony tipped my chin up to meet her eyes. "You should have told us, sweetie. Helen and Willa could have figured something out, but missing two days of homework hurts you a lot."

"I'm sorry. I just wanted to help so much."

"We know you did," M said, joining us in a loosely held hug. "But you need to be honest with us. If we ask about homework or anything that might stop you from doing something you want to do, you have to be honest. We might be able to find a solution that works for everyone. Okay?"

"Yes." The heavy boulder lifted off my stomach. I shouldn't have lied, but I really thought I could get the assignments done this weekend before the teacher talked to me about it. That way I could help Helen and keep my grades up.

"Good." M let out a sigh and rubbed my back.

"Just talk to us from now on, okay?" Briony's hands patted my shoulders. "I don't like doing this, but you broke the rules, so no video games for a week. And you're starting those two homework assignments tonight."

That was it? I lie and flunk two assignments, and she's only taking away video games that are her son's anyway? They weren't going to call my social worker and have me taken to another home for being too much trouble? It was too good to be true.

"Okay," I managed weakly.

Briony hugged me again while M grabbed my duffle bag and tossed it up onto a rack in my closet. I'd never be able to reach it without a step ladder now. M turned back and winked at me, knowing that she'd put the bag out of reach.

"If you need help with the assignments, let us know," Briony told me.

When they left, they kept the door open, which made me feel ten times better. If they'd shut the door, I'd feel like I couldn't leave without permission. One of my other foster families always made us ask to leave our room.

I went right to my desk and pulled out the first assignment I hadn't completed on time. It was a worksheet on sentence construction. After reading, this was the hardest thing for me to figure out. The word order confused me sometimes, but I'd try to get through everything on my own before asking for help.

Three minutes later, Caleb knocked on my open door. He came inside and dropped onto my bed. He did this most nights when he wanted a break from his homework or wanted to talk or wanted to get me to watch TV or play a game with him. He liked to break up his time doing homework. I sometimes joined him, but mostly he just needed a distraction before he'd go back to it.

"Hey," he greeted. "What'd ya do?"

My face got hot. I hated being in trouble.

"Can't be half as bad as when Hank and I snuck a dog we found into the upstairs bathroom for a day without telling them. I'm lucky to have my Xbox back." That sounded like something Hank and Caleb would do.

M could hear a pin drop from another room. There's no way she wouldn't hear a dog upstairs.

"I told them I didn't have any homework so I could keep working with Helen."

He whistled, shaking his head. "Oh, man, lying's a big one for Mom. You could accidently set fire to the entire house and she'd say it's no big deal, but lying gets you punishment every time. What'd you get?"

"A week without video games."

"Bleh," he groaned. "Not fun, but you can make it. We'll play board games or throw a ball around outside instead."

He was so nice, just like his parents. "I thought they'd..."

"What?" he looked curious.

"Nothing." I didn't need to let him know how I thought his parents were going to be like the other families I'd stayed with. I knew they weren't, but I wasn't sure how they'd be if I caused trouble.

"C'mon, tell me." His hand nudged my knee.

"I don't know." I shrugged, but I did know and maybe if I told him it wouldn't be so scary anymore. "Other places would have kicked me out."

He jerked back like my words smacked him or something. "Harsh! No way, Liv. Mom and M would never do that. You're stuck with us."

That sounded great. Better than great. I crossed my fingers, hoping that was true.

6

Briony gripped my hand as we walked downstairs. She took us straight to our bedroom and closed the door behind us. Tears welled in her eyes. "Did you see her? Did you see what she did?"

"Yes." I had. I'd seen almost the exact same thing when I was a kid. Whenever the parents or worse, the social worker, would break the news that it was time to move to another house. Every excuse would be given. They were moving or they lost their jobs or they had a niece who would be coming to live with them and they needed the room back. Whatever the reason, the resignation settled in just as fast as the disappointment. Yes. I'd seen it. I just didn't think Olivia thought that could happen to her here. My head hurt like someone had stomped on it after I'd already been beaten to the ground.

"She thought we were going to make her leave." A tear escaped before Briony wiped it away. "I need a hug."

I held up my arms and she slipped into them. She squeezed tight like she was afraid I'd evaporate. Her lips brushed against my neck as she settled in for what would likely be a hugging marathon.

"This is awful. It feels awful. You didn't warn me that it would feel so awful." She pulled back and stared at me with her golden eyes.

"I know." Dread filled my chest. From the second we got the teacher's phone call, acid seemed to be churning in my stomach. She'd never lied to us, not that we knew of. Other than a minor scolding that usually applied to both kids, we'd never had to discipline her. I knew why. I could see it when we first met her. She would do everything she could to please us. She'd been tossed from one home to the next, seven in all and three temporary group home stays. She volunteered to help, she stayed quiet, and she didn't cause problems, all to avoid having to move again. She'd come out of her shell so far since getting comfortable with us. I hoped this wouldn't make her retreat again.

"Do you? That was just awful."

"I tried to warn you that it wouldn't be all rainbows and puppies. Taking in someone else's child can be difficult, especially when they're older. We've been incredibly fortunate so far." I reached up and tucked the bangs that always fell over one eye behind her ear.

"But why would she think we'd make her leave over something like this? I don't understand. I thought we made her feel at home here. Haven't we done that?"

"That's just the way it is in the foster system." I cupped her cheek. Briony had no experience with feeling unwanted. "She probably liked living at a few other places, but all of a sudden, she gets told she's going to be placed somewhere else. It happens for a lot of reasons."

Briony finally stepped back and pulled on my hand to have me sit beside her on the bed. "Is this hard for you, honey? When we agreed to do this, I didn't think how hard it might be for you."

I drew in a calming breath and let it out. I suspected that offering Olivia a home would bring back some difficult memories. Mostly, though, it's been a lot of joyful recollections about how safe Kathryn had made me feel. She'd taken me in when I'd been ditched as a baby and loved me as her own for my first nine years until she died. For my entire adult life, I'd wanted to provide the same for another girl. I just never felt sure enough of my social abilities until Briony. With her help and love, I could accomplish my dream of giving a safe, caring, happy, and permanent home to a parentless child like I'd been. Based on how Olivia reacted to our first real attempt at discipline tonight, I realized she didn't yet think of our home that way. That didn't sit well with me. Not well at all.

"Mostly it's made me remember how much I adored my time with Kathryn. But, sweetheart," I started, turning to face her fully and gripping both of her hands. "I know this whole foster thing was my idea. You agreed because it was so important to me, but we never really talked about the long term." My throat started closing up. When I first brought up fostering a child, I thought we were on the same page and wanted the same things. Now that it's been several months, she might be thinking something different, and I didn't know how to express just how much I wanted what I was going to ask for.

Briony smoothed her fingers down my cheek. "What are you thinking?"

That I wanted Olivia with us. That I wanted her to experience home again. Not a home like we'd been providing. But home like the place in your heart and head and soul when you think of the best most permanent place you can go. That I wanted it always, but I didn't know how to ask my partner for such a huge want and didn't know what I'd do if she didn't want the same thing. I loved Briony so much, but I couldn't compromise on this.

She gripped my chin and skimmed her lips against mine. "If the next words out of your mouth aren't, 'I want us to adopt her,' I may not speak to you for a whole month."

My eyes flooded and my throat closed completely. Briony was the only person who could do this to me. Before her, I rarely cried, and as happy as she made me, I shouldn't need to cry ever again. But with Briony I'd learned what tears of joy meant.

"You couldn't even make it a full day, sweetheart," I teased and received a hard shove before she righted me and seized my mouth in a demanding kiss.

When she pulled back, her thumb swiped along my lower lip. Her eyes traced the movement like she wanted to follow it with her mouth again. "It would be a really long day for you, M."

"Is that what you want, Bri?" I watched her face for any of the usual signs that she didn't really mean what she was saying. She had one of the best poker faces around.

"To adopt her? Yes, honey, of course. I love that girl." She shook her head and smiled. "I admit when you first suggested the foster program I thought it might not work out, but I knew how important it was for you. When we went through all those program classes, I had a lot of doubts about it. I didn't like the idea of basically being considered a temporary caretaker with no real parental authority. I mean, we can't even let her go on a sleepover. We had to ask four of our friends to get background checks just so we'd have a fallback if we needed a sitter. Even medical care needs to be preapproved by her social worker for anything other than an emergency, and if an emergency ever happened, we'd probably have her taken away from us. It wasn't how I thought it would be."

I threaded my fingers through hers. Everything she'd just said was right and while we liked to think of her as our daughter, we couldn't make long lasting decisions about her. "And now?"

"It hasn't been the glorified babysitting experience they made it out to seem, which I'm very glad about. I'm also glad you were so insistent about who we took in. I honestly don't know what I'd do if she had a parent who was able to come back and take her from us." She shuddered and leaned forward to take me in her arms again.

"You really want to adopt her?" Hope filled my heart.

"Don't you?"

"Very much," I whispered, feeling the relief as if it were a tangible object. I knew I could have talked about it with Briony before this, but I was still getting used to having everything I'd never even thought to dream about.

"I'm so glad you said that," she breathed out. "Do you know how to start the process? Do we talk to a lawyer?"

"Her social worker first."

"Can we tell her now?" She shivered in excitement. "She was so hurt tonight."

I shook my head, not liking that I had to disappoint her. "We need to wait. I know it's exciting, but we need to wait and see if it's possible first. Then we decide when to ask her."

She frowned. "Don't you think she'd want to know?"

"Yes, but I also think that a kid whose first reaction to doing something wrong is that we're going to make her leave may not be in the same place as we are on this. It may be best to wait until school's out."

"That long? Why?" Confusion pinched her beautiful features.

I let out a breath before stating what would be hard to hear. "What if she doesn't want to be adopted?" Briony's confusion deepened. She'd always belonged to a loving family and couldn't imagine voluntarily leaving it. "You know how much she loves her mom. She might think it's a betrayal of that love."

Her eyes widened. "I didn't even think of that."

"If she decides she doesn't want to be adopted, then she may ask to be placed somewhere else. I'd rather her finish the school year before we put her in that position so she doesn't have to change schools if she decides she doesn't want to stay with us."

"Oh God." Panic flashed on her face. "Do you think she doesn't want to be ours?"

I smiled trying to reassure her. "I think she does, but on the small chance that she doesn't, let's be smart about the timing, okay?"

She sighed and brought a hand up to her heart. "I'm so happy you brought her into our lives, but now I'm terrified that she won't want to stay."

"Didn't you always say that parenthood is a combination of happy and terrified at all times?"

"Don't throw my logic back at me when I'm freaking out, M." She pursed her lips and shook her finger at me. "I never thought I'd want another child, especially one who will become the scariest thing on the planet sooner than we can imagine."

I tilted my head in question.

"A teenage girl? There's truly nothing more frightening." She smiled bright enough to light up the whole room. "She's worth it, though."

Yes, she was. The girl who would hopefully become our daughter would be worth any heartache her teenage years might cause.

7

The grocery store wasn't too crowded this morning. I wondered if Briony and Caleb were having the same luck. Olivia and I wandered through the empty aisles selecting our groceries for the week. Months ago, Briony and I decided to split the errands on weekends to keep the kids from getting too bored. It worked well enough, but on busy weeks like we'd just had, it meant less time with my partner on the weekends.

"Hi there, M."

I turned to find Lauren pushing a full cart down the aisle toward us. She wore a bright smile that competed with her bright red hair. Almost always bubbly, Lauren took a little getting used to when I'd first started seeing Briony. Nothing as bad as some of her other friends, but I'd wanted to like Lauren immediately because of how she was and who she was in the group. I made every effort to drop my defenses around her.

"Hi, Lauren," I greeted.

She nodded and touched Olivia's shoulder. "Hi, Livy. It's nice to run into someone I like today."

"Uh-oh," I murmured, wondering who else she'd seen this morning.

"Jessie keeps telling me to represent less skeevy people so I won't mind seeing clients around town" She chuckled at her joke. "What are you up to today? Got any big plans?" She directed her question at Olivia, which was one of the things I liked about Lauren and Jessie. They talked to the kids, not at them or around them whenever we all got together. They were always offering to sit the kids if Briony and I needed a night out. They didn't even bat an eye when we told them it would require a background check. For that reason, I tried very hard to be as social as I could with Lauren.

"Willa invited us over for a swim," Olivia told her, looking every bit the clone of Lauren's bubbliness.

"How fun."

"What is, honeybun?" Lauren's mom asked as she walked up behind her with a carton of eggs. In her eighties, she still seemed as spritely as her daughter whenever I saw them together. "Oh, hello, dearies," she greeted us. "I heard you're going to be a chef, sweet girl."

Olivia's eyes grew wide. She looked over at me. I brought my hand up to cradle the back of her neck showing the support that Briony always showed me in social situations. All it took was a brief touch to calm the panic I could work myself into around people.

"Helen wouldn't stop talking about how talented you are," Lauren told her. "I think she's planned out your entire career for you."

Olivia smiled and laughed nervously, stepping closer to me. She wasn't okay being the center of attention either.

"Knowing Helen, she won't wait until you're done with culinary school, Livy," Rena told us.

"She won't even wait until you're done with high school," Lauren joked and looked at me. "One day you might come home from work and find a kayak in

Olivia's room. It'll be a nice kayak, one that Helen's husband made by hand, but it'll be a kayak instead of a child with only a note telling you she's recruited Olivia for her restaurant."

"Oh, you," Rena brushed off her daughter's tease. "Now listen, sweet girl, if you want to learn how to make an Irish feast, you come see me."

"Take her up on it. Nobody makes corned beef and cabbage like Mom," Lauren bragged.

"How's your husband feeling, Rena?" I asked to steer the attention away from Olivia.

"He's doing better, thanks. His hip is almost healed and we're spoiled rotten living with our daughters like we are."

Lauren slipped an arm around her mom. "Jessie and I are the spoiled ones, Mom."

"Don't let Cap hear you say that or we'll never leave."

"Fine by me," Lauren told her. Warmth bloomed in my chest. This was exactly how I'd imagined interacting with Kathryn if she'd lived past my ninth birthday. "So a little swim fun today?" Lauren turned back to us.

Olivia nodded as I confirmed verbally. Willa offered her pool as a warm weather destination for our family whenever we wanted. Briony and I decided we wouldn't take advantage of that offer too much over the summer break. It might be ideal, but we'd stick to occasional days when both Quinn and Willa were at work to keep from becoming a nuisance. For now, we were happy to accept an invitation if Willa was on her own for the weekend because Quinn was off on a recruiting trip.

"You girls have fun," Rena said and patted Olivia's shoulder. "We'll figure out a night when you can come over for dinner."

We continued on with our shopping as they made their turn out of the aisle. Olivia waited a full minute before she glanced up at me. "Could we really go over for dinner or was she just being polite?"

I pulled in a breath, surprised by her request. She was usually very shy around the group of friends. I knew she liked cooking, but this was brave for her. "I'm pretty sure she meant it. If you want to learn, we'll make it happen." I gave her shoulder an encouraging squeeze. "Do you think that might be something you want to do when you're older? A chef like Helen?"

"Maybe. I like it a lot." She shrugged but shot a quick glance at me. "What do you think?"

"I think you can do anything you want to do, Liv." She could; she just needed the reinforcement until she felt secure enough to know it for herself.

She blushed and turned back to our grocery list. "Should we get the ingredients for Helen's rosemary chicken?"

"You're the chef, kiddo."

"Yo, what's going on?" Caleb called out as he jogged down the aisle toward us. "We finished already. What's taking you so long? We've got some swimming to do."

"Hold your horses there, bucko." Briony came to a stop behind him. She stroked a hand over Olivia's head and leaned in for a peck from me. "We're not invited until this afternoon, and we've still got errands to do."

"Drop me and Liv off at Willa's first. She'll be okay with it. She loves us."

I hid my smile behind a fist. What would that be like? To be so sure of someone's love when she wasn't even a relative? It felt wonderful to know that I was part of a family that provided that kind of security for kids.

"She might love you, but that won't keep her from drowning you when you get on her nerves." Briony's hands gripped his shoulders and shook him as if to knock some sense into him.

"Ha-ha. I can swim and she'd never try it in front of Livy."

We both laughed at his reasoning. Briony shook her head at him. "We're invited over at two; we're getting there at two. As you get older, you'll realize that weekends aren't always about fun."

"Yeah, yeah," he sighed and looped an arm around Olivia's shoulders. "C'mon, let's go pick out the good cereal."

"If sugar is the first ingredient, it's going right back on the shelf!" Briony called after them. She turned back to me. "Think we could get Willa to keep him for his teenage years while we hold onto Olivia? I'm afraid he's going to warp her permanently."

I chuckled and slid an arm around her. "He'll keep us young."

"More like age us rapidly."

"Did you get everything on your list?"

"All set. You almost done here?"

"Just a couple more things. We ran into Lauren and her mom. They invited Olivia to be Rena's assistant chef for a night. She seemed pretty jazzed about it."

"Rena or Olivia?" Briony smiled.

"Both, I think. Olivia admitted she might want to become a chef when she grows up."

Briony's eyes grew wide. "That's great, isn't it? That's she's admitting to a future and one influenced by someone in our lives?"

I nodded as the relief I could see on Briony's face transferred to me. We'd been trying for months to get Olivia to think long term with us, to think long term period. The foster system can mess with that type of planning sometimes, but we'd hoped to provide an environment different than what she'd felt in the past.

It had taken me a while to get to that point in my life, but it was made infinitely easier once I learned to trust my feelings for this wonderful woman next to me.

8

Olivia Sixth grade must have been designed as a cruel joke. Too old for elementary school, too young for junior high. Caleb didn't complain about seventh grade, so this school thing had to get better. Hopefully so would the kids because these sixth grade girls were like panda bears, deceptively cute looking but viscous wild animals underneath.

I passed one of the girl packs on my way to my usual waiting place. I snuck a glance at them and tried to remember if I'd ever seen any of them walking alone. Krystal and her pack were never separated. As much as I wanted a good friend, I didn't think I could get used to needing someone to walk everywhere with me. What did they do over the summer? I grinned when I thought about them cowering in their rooms because they were too afraid to walk anywhere alone.

The smile flattened quickly when I thought about my summer. Summer wasn't my favorite time. Families decided they needed to move or went on vacations or got bad grade reports and decided they didn't want their foster kids anymore. My grades got me sent to a temporary home then on to the group home last summer where I stayed until October when Briony and M came by. They always included me in this year's summer plans. They even talked about my birthday, which wasn't until August. It made me feel like I could believe them when they said they wouldn't ask me to leave.

"Hey, retard!" Krystal shouted from inside another clump of girls. The huddle burst into cackles of laughter.

I froze, still not used to her new favorite taunt. My eyes shot to where the teachers were helping the little kids load into the right cars. The screeching excitement of the kids kept them from hearing Krystal, and she knew it. I used to like getting out of class early, but that just gave girls like Krystal more time to make someone's life sucky. It looked like it was my turn again today.

"Maybe she's too stupid to understand you," Kortney said and the minions laughed with her.

"Maybe you're too much of a jerk for her to want to talk to you," a voice shouted just as loudly.

My head whipped around to see the new kid marching across the courtyard to push through the passel and stand directly in front of Krystal and Kortney. She'd shown up in our class two weeks ago and hadn't yet eaten in the cafeteria at lunch. I suspected she took a bag lunch out onto the grounds and ate alone. If not for a couple of the fifth graders who let me sit at their table, I'd probably do the same thing.

"What's it to you, new girl...or boy? Which is it? Can't you make up your mind?" Krystal sneered at her.

I cringed. That was really bad, too. The new girl had short black hair, not much longer than a boy's cut, and she almost always wore jeans, t-shirts, and work boots. She didn't look girly, but then not everyone had developed like Krystal and her friends. Their bra sizes were the worst kept secret in our class. I didn't even have a training bra yet, but with my long hair no one mistook me for a boy.

"Blockheads," she said to them and started walking away.

"Don't you know?" Krystal taunted. "Or are you one of those freaks that is both?"

The girl turned back to her and smiled, not fake at all, like she was having fun talking to these mean girls. "I know exactly who I am, and I feel sorry for you. The only way you can feel good about yourself is to put others down."

"If she's a boy, she's a girly boy." Krystal ignored the very smart thing the girl said.

She scoffed then turned away and started walking toward me. I was still frozen in place, my eyes searching for a place to hide.

"Oh, look, girl-boy freak is friends with retard freak. They're a perfect match," Krystal shouted and pointed.

My mouth nudged open. I didn't think it was possible for her to get any meaner.

"Sorry." The new girl stopped in front of me. She was a good six inches taller than me and her dark brown eyes were bright and untroubled. "They're jerks."

I nodded, surprised that her tone was easygoing. Like it didn't bother her at all that the girls were making fun of her.

"I'm Eden, you're Olivia, right?"

She must know my name because Mrs. Lomax liked calling on me in class more than the other kids. I was pretty sure the teacher did it to show everyone how much I didn't know. It was the same treatment for the two boys who always acted like class clowns. I never acted up, but it didn't seem to matter to the teacher. "Yep."

"Come on, let's go sit on the wall over there." She pointed to a place far away from Krystal's group. "My dad's coming to pick me up if you need a ride home."

She tugged on my arm, which didn't really give me a choice, but for once I didn't mind. Krystal was still yammering about something. It was so much easier to ignore her when someone else was there.

"You should have seen this jerk at my last school. Krystal's easy compared to him." She sat on the edge of the wall and looked off toward where the cars come into the parking lot to pick us up. "My dad says to feel sorry for them, but sometimes it's hard."

I nodded again. It sure was hard. I didn't feel sorry for Krystal or any of her friends. I just wanted all of them to leave me alone.

"Have you always gone to school here?" she asked me.

"No."

"Do you like it here?"

I shrugged, not sure how to answer. I loved living with M and Briony, but I didn't like Krystal and she wasn't moving any time soon.

"You don't talk much, do you?" She grinned, showing a little gap between her two front teeth. "That's okay. My dad says I talk enough for everyone around me."

I laughed, which surprised me. Usually only Caleb could make me laugh after Krystal picked on me.

"Is that your mom?" Eden pointed toward the parking lot. M was getting out of her car, her eyes on me, smiling.

For a second I wished I could say yes. I really liked M, even let myself start to love her, and it would make things so much easier. But she wasn't and I felt guilty for wishing she was. I had a mom, a great mom.

"No."

Eden stiffened and stood as M began walking toward us. "Do you know her?"

I frowned at where she stood, blocking me from seeing M. "Yes."

Eden relaxed and sat back down. "Like a sitter or something?"

I shook my head and frowned again. I hated telling people I was in foster care. Kids really didn't get it. "I stay with her."

"Hi, Olivia. You got out early, huh?" M stopped in front of me. She smiled at Eden. "Hello, I'm M."

Eden brightened and waved. "Hi, I'm Eden."

"Nice to meet you, Eden. How long for Caleb and Hank?" M looked at her watch. She knew exactly when they'd be out of class, but she needed something to talk about. She didn't talk much either.

"A couple minutes."

"Are they your brothers?" Eden asked me. "I've got three. They're all in high school. I was the big surprise."

M chuckled. "Do you need a ride home, Eden?"

"No thanks. My dad's coming by to take me to his jobsite today. He's a plumber. I'm helping him for the rest of the school year because my brothers are all freaking out about their finals right now."

"That's a skill that will always come in handy," M commented as she watched the doors on the middle school across the street open and a stream of kids flow out.

It got a lot louder. M and I usually just waited quietly until Caleb and Hank found us, but today, Eden chattered on. It was kind of a fun change.

"Hey," Caleb called out. Hank waved his hello.

"Hi, guys," M said and signed at the same time. She was as good at signing as Hank was. She'd been teaching me since I came to live with them because Hank was always over at the house. The weirdest thing was, sometimes I thought it was easier to speak in sign language than it was out loud. "Do you know Eden?"

"Hey, Eden," they both said because they were real friendly like that.

Eden chatted to them as easily as she would her own brothers. M watched us closely. She'd noticed it, too, but she noticed everything.

"You guys should take off before the parking lot gets too crowded to get out of here," Eden told M.

"We're in no hurry, are we, guys?" M asked.

In response, Hank and Caleb dropped onto the grass next to us, ready to stay as long as necessary. I didn't want to leave Eden alone with Krystal and her gang still hanging around. M wasn't about to leave her alone either. Not that she knew about Krystal, but M was super protective.

"Cool." Eden settled back beside me on the wall. "Hey, you didn't say. Are these guys your brothers?" Her fingers waved at Caleb and Hank.

My shoulders dropped. I'd have to tell her.

"I am," Caleb said and smacked Hank. "He might as well be."

"Yep," Hank added.

I was too shocked to speak. I guess Caleb must be getting tired of explaining who I was to his friends. I looked up at M, expecting to see her shock. Instead, she was smiling and acting like what he said was perfectly fine. I'd lived in some homes where the foster parents insisted we call them Mom and Dad and all the other kids our brothers and sisters, but M and Briony never made me do that.

"Cool." Eden accepted it easily. "You have any sisters?"

I shook my head. I didn't have any brothers either, but it was nice that Caleb thought I was kinda like a sister. He treated me better than a sister, or at least the way I'd seen brothers in other homes treat their sisters.

"Me, neither, but I always get my own room. Two of my brothers share at home and all three have to share at my mom's. Makes them so mad." She started laughing like it was fun to make her brothers mad.

"Nice," Caleb reached back for a high five from her.

"There's my dad." Eden pointed to the pickup pulling into the parking lot. She sprang off the wall ready to race over to him. "Nice meeting ya. See you Monday, Olivia."

"Bye," I called as she sprinted off to his truck.

"She's cool," Hank signed to me, and Caleb nodded.

I smiled, wondering if I'd made a real friend. Then I looked at Caleb, wishing for real that he was my brother. The longer I stayed with them, the more I wished for what I thought were impossible things.

9

Olivia The class was getting loud, but M just kept scribbling on the white board. If this were my class, our teacher would be yelling at us to be quiet. M didn't teach her classes that way. She let her students speak up, talk to each other during class, and encouraged discussion when she was teaching. It wasn't like our class where Mrs. Lomax talked and we listened. M asked her students questions and let them carry the discussion by themselves if they wanted. If I had a teacher like M, I'd love school.

She turned back from the board, and the students settled down instantly. I didn't really understand what today's subject was, but I liked listening. Based on the number of people in M's classes, she was really popular. Briony teased her about it all the time. Briony's students really liked her, too, but she never had classes this size.

"What about output efficiency techniques?" M asked to no one in particular. That was another thing that was different from my teacher. Mrs. Lomax would call on someone. If they didn't know the answer, she wouldn't just let them off the hook. It could get really embarrassing.

One of the guys in front started talking without raising his hand. M let them get away with it as long as they weren't interrupting someone else. After he finished talking, M asked the rest of the class if that made sense. That was M's way of getting the class to tell him he was wrong instead of her telling him outright.

She started up the steps to where I sat at her desk. M moved around a lot in her classroom. She told me it kept people from texting in class or whispering to each other and kept their attention focused. Her desk was up on the third row of the eight rows of seating. I wasn't sure why she didn't have her desk down at the front of the room, but it was probably for some really good teaching reason.

A stack of stapled paper sets sat neatly on the corner of her desk. Her eyes landed on them and looked back at me with a smile. She didn't need to ask, but she whispered, "Would you mind passing these out, please?"

I stood and picked up the stack of papers on her desk. Whenever she needed something handed out, she'd ask me to do it. She thought I got bored just sitting here. Once a month my school had half days, so M would come pick me up and bring me back for her last class. Briony did the same when she was on pickup duty. Hank's grandmother would pick up the boys at the normal time. I didn't mind coming back to work with them. Their students were entertaining, and it was neat to see them teach.

Heading up to the top row, I counted out the handouts and gave them to the first girl sitting there. She smiled at me, over smiled, really. Some of M's students did that with me because they thought they could kiss up to their professor if they were nice to me. They all thought I was M's kid because she didn't really tell them who I was when she introduced me the first time.

"Thanks, Olivia," M said as I got down to the bottom row. "You've just been handed a case study on a now defunct manufacturing company. Work in groups of four or five to get this analysis done by next Wednesday. We'll see where you're at on Monday. That's class for today, guys. Be safe out there."

Half the class bolted for the door, but the rest went to surround M and ask questions. Normally it would only be a few people, but she must have given them something harder today. Since I was done with my homework already, I sat back in M's desk chair and pulled out a library book to read. It was about a teen who'd been made into a tour guide hologram for Disney World and finds out many of the evil characters are real and trying to break out of Disney to take over the world. Caleb recommended it. He was already on the fourth in the series. I liked the other series he told me to get about triplet decedents of Medusa better, but I finished those. Before M's house, I never read anything for fun because it was so hard and I didn't know how to find something good. But trips to the library were a regular occurrence for this family. So was reading a chapter before bed every night. M had shown me some tricks to help me read better, like looking at the first and last letters and length of the word instead of trying to string all the letters together when they seemed to jump around on me. She got me to focus on the pattern of a word, not all the letters and now I always carried a book to read for fun.

"What're you reading?" one of the guys in the class asked me as he dropped an assignment on M's desk. I glanced up and showed him the cover of the book. "Read that one. It's pretty good. You'll like the ending."

"Don't spoil it for her, Joel," M called out as she waved off the rest of the people surrounding her and made her way up the tiered rows to her desk.

"I wasn't, Prof," he protested, holding his hands up. "Just thought she'd like to know that the kid gets—"

"Joel!" M snapped at him.

He started laughing really hard, like getting M to snap at him was his goal. "Just kidding," he said to me. "Must be fun living with Prof."

"Get out of here," M said in a stern tone that wasn't really all that stern.

He sauntered out just as Briony appeared in the doorway. She looked exhausted as she usually did on Wednesdays when she had department meetings.

"My two favorite people." Briony walked toward us and gave M a kiss before leaning down to kiss the top of my head. Other foster parents would kiss my cheek or head and all I'd want to do was wipe away the spot. I never felt that way with them.

"How was the meeting?" M asked her.

"Useless, as always. Remind me why I decided to accept a chair position?"

"Because you're good at it?" I guessed because we all had to be positive for Briony on department meeting days.

"Because you thought it would come with a really nice chair?" M joked and got a smack to the shoulder for it.

Briony slipped her arm around me. "What do you two have planned for your girls' night? You sure you don't want to join Lex, Javi, and me?"

"Nope, you have fun with your friends," M told her. "You don't get a night out with them alone often, and Liv and I have big plans."

"What?" Briony's eyes sparkled with interest.

"You'll find out."

I knew it wouldn't be something that Briony would be mad she missed. That wasn't how they treated each other. Other families would get into huge fights when one person got to spend a night out and the other one was stuck with the kids. Especially if that person spent all of their money for the week at a bar. Briony wouldn't do that, and M liked hanging out with Caleb and me as much as her adult friends.

"No secrets now," Briony goaded, reaching out to tickle M.

"You'll just have to wait to be jealous of our fun." M shuffled away from Briony's fingers.

"I should join your girls' night."

"You should, but Alexa won't let you out and Javier needs you to help rein her in."

I snickered. Alexa and Javier, two other professors, acted like an old married couple without being a couple. They were funny together and always talked directly to me like the best of Briony and M's friends. They were like Willa, Quinn, Jessie, and Lauren who didn't treat me like I was six and a sad little orphan. Or worse like they couldn't understand why Briony and M would want me to live with them. It wasn't like their other friends weren't nice to me. It was just that some of them didn't understand why someone would foster when they could have their own kids.

"Oh, you think that's funny, do you, missy?" Briony's teasing smile turned toward me, her fingers spread out for attack. Tickling was her special torture for Caleb and me.

I ducked behind M, giggling. This no longer reminded me of my mom who used to tickle me. Now I only thought of the times Briony surprised me or Caleb or especially M with her tickle fingers.

"Enough fun, sweetheart." M pulled her away from me before I started crying from laughing so hard. "You'd better get moving if you don't want those two tracking you down in the hallways. It's always so much worse if they have to come find you."

Briony's smile went from teasing to tender when she looked into M's eyes. My stomach got warm tingles whenever I saw proof of how much they loved each other. I'd lived in two homes with single parents and five homes with married people. Briony and M haven't been married very long, so maybe that's why they still loved each other. The other couples didn't even seem to like each other anymore. Some of them thought that fighting was their entertainment for the evening. I'd never heard Briony and M fight. They didn't agree on everything, but they found a middle ground pretty quickly.

Briony slid her arms around M's waist. She gave her a another kiss. Caleb sometimes gets embarrassed by any affection they showed, but I didn't mind.

"I love you," she whispered then took a step back and looked at me. "I love you, too, sweetie." She reached an arm over and dragged me into a group hug. "You girls have fun tonight."

I turned to M and smiled, happier than I'd been in a really long time. We had nights out alone at least once a month. Then Briony would get pretend jealous and make up a reason for us to have a night out alone. They did the same with Caleb, but it always made me feel super special when they'd take me somewhere by myself.

"Are you ready?" M asked me, reaching for her computer bag.

"What are we doing?" I bounced on my toes waiting to hear.

"The community center is sponsoring a cooking class at our favorite Greek restaurant. They're teaching their secrets to the best gyros, which will make Caleb our grateful servant when we add it to the dinner rotation. What do you think?"

"Ooh, yeah, please. That sounds really fun. Are you sure you'll like it?" I had to ask because M didn't cook dinner often. She usually took care of breakfast and made sandwiches for lunch, but unless she was grilling, Briony did most of the dinner cooking.

"Sure, I will. It'll be fun with you." She slid an arm around my shoulder and squeezed briefly. She didn't often show affection like this, but I didn't ever feel like I missed it. She made sure we all knew how much she cared for us. "Let's go have some fun."

I wanted to thank her and call her Mom because this was something only a mother would do for her child, but she hadn't said I should. Those other families who forced us to call them Mom and Dad did it so we'd feel included. But I always felt like it disrespected my mom. Now that I'd been with Briony and M for eight months, I wanted to call them Mom or Momma or something that signified how much they meant to me. When they did things like this for me, over and above giving me a home, food, and clothing, I wouldn't feel guilty that I wanted them to be my real parents. My mom wouldn't mind because they were so good to me and loved me. I was sure she'd be happy about it.

10

Morning sunlight filtered through the teal curtains in our bedroom. The growing heat and brightness woke me fully. Briony slept on beside me. Her hand lay on my shoulder, something she did throughout the night as if she had to stay connected to me at all times.

I rolled onto my side and studied my partner. I loved being able to say that, loved having a partner. For someone as damaged as I'd been, I never even hoped to be in this position.

Wheat blond hair brushed forward over her neck and pushed out behind her on the pillow. My fingers came up to drift down her neck, the skin soft and warm beneath my touch. I traced a path down to the straps of the camisole she was wearing and onto her shoulder.

"Morning," her husky voice broke my concentration. She tilted toward me and stretched, her golden eyes blinking in the morning light.

"Good morning." I watched her morning ritual with all the fascination I'd given it the first time we spent the night together.

She smiled and cocked her head, listening for any other sounds of life in the house. It was still a half hour before one of the kids would usually be up. Her smile flared when she didn't hear anything. Her stretch lengthened, pushing me onto my back so she could cover me with her whole body.

"Hello," I smiled up at her. My hands gripped her hips then skimmed up her sides, dipping under the camisole to appreciate her lean torso better.

She dropped a kiss on my mouth. "God, it feels like ages since I've had my hands on you."

"It's only been a week." Last Saturday night to be precise when both Caleb and Olivia were sound asleep by nine-thirty after a long day of indoor laser tag. My laughter died in a groan when her mouth dragged down my throat.

"A very long week." Her lips traced the angle of my V-neck shirt. Her hands ducked under the hem and pushed upward. "You feel better each time I touch you."

I brought her camisole up and forced her mouth away from me to get it off. I took advantage of her raised position and ran my hands up the front of her to cup her breasts. I could never get enough of them. My thumbs swiped over the pale pink buds, bringing them to erect points.

She hissed and swooped down to kiss me. Soft lips and a surging tongue stoked the embers in my stomach. Her hands eagerly pushed at my t-shirt to bare my chest and mimic my caresses. A thigh dipped in between my legs and pushed against my suddenly throbbing center. Before Briony I'd never felt these sensations before. Now, in less than a minute, I could go from tranquil to desperately needy.

I reached down to strip off her shorts and let my hands skate back up over her rear. Desperation fueled my touch, but it warred with the need to drag it out. My breath was already ragged as I strained up against her thigh. Her fingers pulled at my underwear. I helped, frantic to slide my hot skin against hers.

Kisses rained down my chest, headed exactly where I needed. Her lips sucked my nipple into her mouth. My back arched off the mattress, following the suction of her lips. Her masterful tongue lapped and teased. It wasn't until her husky chuckle that I remembered I had hands and a mouth of my own.

The chuckle died in her throat as my fingers grasped her nipples and tweaked just so. "Oh, yes, M," she moaned as I repeated the maneuver. "Just like that."

Her mouth was still making me brainless, but I knew we didn't have all morning. Leisurely lovemaking had to be left to the nights when the kids were already in bed. A stolen morning meant fast, sometimes hard, but always explosive.

I slid a hand down her side and over her lower back, adding pressure to bring her fully onto me. Her pelvis fit to mine, both legs slipping between my thighs. Her face turned up to look at me with a sexy fire lighting her eyes. She circled her hips against me, fierce and powerful grinding. Little puffs of air pushed against my lips with her efforts.

Thunder sounded in rhythmic pounds from above, halting our motions. If I didn't know better I'd think a large animal herd was coming down the stairs instead of just one boy. I sighed and Briony groaned.

"Cross your fingers he can entertain himself," I whispered and rolled my pelvis against hers again.

"I did thank you for insisting we add sound insulation to the bedrooms and bathrooms when we renovated, didn't I?" Her eyes twinkled down at me.

I felt a blush bloom on my cheeks remembering how Des had reacted when I asked for the insulation on the interior walls. I'd done it as much for the necessary quiet I needed to sleep as for the privacy we'd need to talk without Caleb overhearing and for moments like this. Nothing would embarrass me more if Briony's son or our foster daughter could hear us making love.

I tunneled my hand between us and cupped her, effectively ending her tease. She was wet and plump and gorgeous in my hand. She wouldn't last long. After years of making love with her, I could sense her climax almost before she could.

A knock sounded at the door. "Mom? You up yet?" Caleb's raised voice reached us through the solid wood of the bedroom door. "We're out of pancake mix."

Briony gave a long, loud groan. He might have heard that one. "I'll be there in a minute," she called back, stilling her hips and shoving up onto stiff arms. She shook her head and gave me an apologetic look. "Dammit."

I chuckled at her exasperation. We'd been interrupted before, but like she said, it had been a long week. She moved to get up, but my hands gripped her in place. I shook my head and gave her a determined look. My fingers went to work.

"We don't have enough time," she whispered and moaned as I zeroed in on her engorged clit.

"You're almost there." Adding the pressure she always needed to climax, I circled with one finger before sliding my hand lower. Her hips tilted automatically, seeking and needing what we both wanted. I didn't make her wait. My index and middle fingers plunged into her silky depths. If we had more time, I would have drawn it out, slipping one then another inside her. Her moan told me she didn't mind my hastiness. I pumped into her with my hips. She rocked against me, letting breathy sounds escape her lips against my ear. I added a thumb to her clit, rubbing just right. "You need this, Bri. Come for me."

Her hips thrust hard against my hand. She leaned down to take my mouth in a savage kiss that was both demanding and preventative in keeping her usual exclamations from escaping. I felt the telltale flutters around my thrusting fingers before she went rigid and contractions squeezed my fingers to the sound of her muffled groan.

Her body dropped onto me in a boneless heap as her breath brushed over my neck. Nothing felt better than satisfying the woman I loved. "That was…God, Mabel." She didn't seem to have the energy to finish the thought.

I smiled at her sated state. Sparks raced through me every time she used my name. I never liked it, even when Kathryn called me by the name she'd chosen. But now, in these private moments with my partner, one whispered "Mabel" and I'd feel like I was falling in love all over again.

My hands rubbed her smooth back. This always reenergized her. She'd shift and shudder, milking the back rub for every second. Truthfully, I could stay in this position for hours, but we didn't have that luxury.

"Let me," she began, hands drifting down my sides.

I stopped their movement. "Not enough time. Somebody needs to be talked out of pancakes."

"That kid!" she complained mockingly. "Here's the deal. I'll get French toast started and join you in the shower where we can finish this."

I nodded, not counting on her being able to keep the promise because that was the life of a parent. As she pulled on her camisole, I found her shorts and reached for the robe she kept on one of the chairs in our room. I'd lounge here for ten minutes before getting up. Saturdays took some reserve energy to get through.

An hour later, the kids were fed and those special shower promises had been kept. I was still tingling from the refreshing wake up and made a note to set the alarm early for next Saturday so we could start the day the same way.

Caleb finished loading the dishwasher and turned it on. "Whose turn is it today?" He asked this every Saturday morning, even when he knew it wasn't his turn. He always hoped that we'd forget that it wasn't his turn and let him choose.

"Olivia's," Briony told him in a tone that said she knew exactly what he was trying.

This had been a routine she set up with Caleb after his other mom died. Briony put a lot of emphasis on doing activities together that didn't involve a television or game monitor and helped to widen his interests. Family time could be anything from throwing a Frisbee at the park to painting mugs at a pottery store to bike rides and countless other little activities that didn't break the bank. It taught the kids to make their own fun without the aid of television or gossiping with friends.

Changing my usual quiet Saturday plans had been one of those adjustments that worked out well and made me feel like a more complete person for it. I'd always been happy to hibernate on the weekends to decompress and maybe hang out with Willa or help out Hank and Lucille with something around their house. Having to come up with group activities that hopefully everyone would enjoy turned out not to be the pressure cooker I worried it would.

"Six Flags," Caleb tried to mask his suggestion behind a cough.

We all laughed because he said this every weekend even when it was his mom's turn to pick. Olivia would never ask for something like that because she was very aware of the cost of things. I understood where she was coming from but didn't want it to be an issue. Once we adopted her, and I was now almost certain she'd let us, we'd work on getting her to be more of a kid than an accountant.

I waited for her choice. She'd only just begun to pick things she really liked. In the first few months, she'd pick something one of us would always pick like she was afraid that if she decided on an activity that only she liked, we'd have a reason to make her leave.

"Rollerblading," she said, and while she knew it was one of my favorite things to do, it had become one of her favorites, too.

"Rad! Can Hank come with us?" Caleb asked his mom and ran toward the phone as soon as she gave her usual nod. "Livy, phone for you," he called out from the kitchen. We all stared at each other because we hadn't heard the phone ring and no one had ever called for Olivia.

She cautiously made her way over to the phone. I tried not to listen in on her private conversation, but it was plucking my curiosity to know who called. Briony seemed to be leaning toward the conversation as well.

"Hi, Eden."

My heart pumped faster. I'd never have guessed that seeing my child so happy would transfer that happiness to me. She finally had a friend in her own class. Sure, she knew some of the kids to talk to them, but when I used to listen to her day, I'd want to strangle some of the kids at her school.

I stepped up to her and whispered, "Does Eden want to come with us?"

Her eyes popped. She looked grateful that she could invite her friend and relieved that she didn't have to ask permission to make the offer.

Briony stopped beside me, gesturing for the phone. "We need to ask her mom first."

"Dad," I corrected, remembering Eden's situation. Since our first meeting, we'd learned a little more about her divorced parents and her mom's overseas executive job that didn't give her much time with the kids. For a girl who didn't see her mom often, she was terribly well adjusted. Her dad must be a super parent.

Briony nodded and told Olivia, "Her dad has to say it's okay, and I want to hear it from him."

This was where Briony's extra practice as a parent came in handy. It didn't occur to me that we'd need to make sure he was okay with her joining us today. I knew how careful we'd be with her, but of course, he didn't know us yet so this step would be important. I'd learned a lot about parenting from Briony and everything about being part of a family from her. To see Olivia feeling secure, Caleb eager and ready, and Briony happy and serene, I'd gladly give up my once relaxed Saturdays and so much more.

11

One hour into gardening, the kids were ready to quit. Caleb and Hank were already complaining and Olivia looked wiped out. We'd gotten up early so that we could get this yard work done before the heat of late May overwhelmed us. It wasn't how I wanted to spend my last weekend before spring semester ended either, but Lucille needed this done and we were five able-bodied people who could do it.

"It's so hot," Caleb whined.

"Can't we do this another day?" Hank signed.

"We've already put it off the last two weekends because you guys whined about it then," I told them.

"We're not whiners!" Caleb whined again.

I gave him a look. We'd both had to adjust to being part of the same family, and while he could sometimes get away with procrastinating or not doing what he was told with his mom, I tended to wear him down until he did whatever it was.

Olivia was making good progress at clipping the hedges along the fence line, but the boys were dragging their jobs out like they hoped everything would magically get done without them having to work. Lucille had been shaping the ivy, but at sixty-four she actually needed the breaks the two whining teenagers kept asking for.

"I don't see why I couldn't go with Mom today."

I stopped sawing through the dogwood branch I was working on and came out from under the tree to talk to them. As his stepmom, I usually took a reasoning approach with Caleb. Briony could get away with telling him off.

"That wasn't an option," I began. "Our friend asked us for our help. No one likes doing this kind of work in this kind of weather, but we do it because it needs to be done. Does that make sense?" That was my best impression of a reasonable parent.

"Why isn't Mom here helping, then?" Caleb persisted. These kinds of conversations were the first signs he'd turned into a teenager a couple of months ago.

"Your mom has department evaluations to finish and then she's going to Caroline's."

"We could have done that."

I shook my head and sighed. "Because spending an hour with a screaming baby is better than yard work?"

He scoffed and looked like he was going to backtalk again but realized he did get the better option. Sitting quietly in Briony's office while she finished her work and then going over to the new parents' house wouldn't appeal to any teenager. "Can't we take a break?"

"We'll take a lot of breaks before we're done, big guy. For now, Olivia's almost done with the hedge line and you guys have barely started ripping out those dead plants. When you're done with that, we'll take a break."

"With sprinklers?" Hank asked.

Lucille banged open the screen door and said, "Smoothies, but only if the chatter stops."

Olivia giggled as her clippers came closer to where I was standing. "I don't mind switching if they want to." Because that was the kind of sweet kid she was.

"They need to finish what they started, darling," Lucille told her. "When you're done with the hedge, we'll start making the smoothies and see how much longer it takes them to finish."

Olivia smiled and went back to her task. I reached up and put my shoulders into the sawing motion to get this limb down. After storing it in the recycling bin, I headed over to the porch where Lucille had taken a seat. She was fiddling with the flower bed beside her, taking a break while not really taking a break.

"Thank you for doing this, M."

"Anytime, Lucille. You know that."

"Should we try this another day?" Her blue eyes were studying the dragging movements of her grandson.

I shook my head. "After Caleb's birthday, we decided to start making him use more of his free time for chores or work or something that isn't what he wants to do every moment he wants to do it. We think it's the best way to instill a sense of responsibility and make him understand that part of being an adult means you've got to do a lot of things you don't want to."

"A good plan, indeed. I should start the same thing with Hank. He's been getting more and more lippy of late."

"Same with Caleb," I confided. "Briony's good at handling it, but I just keep looking for ways to cut it off before it progresses to what could become shouting matches in a few years."

"It's unavoidable, my dear," Lucille told me. "Both my kids were right as rain until they turned sixteen.

You don't remember, but you were probably the same way."

No, I wasn't. I didn't have the opportunity. I'd spent my high school years in a detention home for kids who would otherwise be sentenced to juvenile hall but because of the precipitating act were sent to an educational-slash-reform facility. The emphasis was on reform as evidenced by the barbed wire fences, locked dorm rooms, forced labor, and zero liberties. Getting lippy there wouldn't have resulted in screaming matches. More work, missed meals, or transfers to juvie were how they dealt with lippy teenagers.

"I plan to have Carlton stop by more often when it starts getting really bad. Hank seems to drop any attitude whenever his uncle is around."

That could happen with role models of the same gender. Briony had already thought about it, which was why Caleb had been spending most of his summers at or near his grandparents' homes so he could spend time with his grandfathers and uncles.

This summer was going to be a challenge. Since Olivia couldn't leave the state without permission, the plan this summer was to send the kids to soccer day camp here. I hoped it wouldn't be more cause for Caleb to act up. He'd have Javier as his assistant coach and Briony and me around more each day. Hopefully that would be enough to quell this recent angst of his. I doubted it would make him drop some of his more lazy tendencies, but it might help him feel more secure.

Other than hoping Olivia would accept our wishes to become part of the family officially, I didn't have any worries about her attitude or behavior. At least not yet. Both Briony and Lucille seemed to think that would change in a few years, but I wasn't too worried. My guess was that she'd always remember her experiences in those other foster homes, and while she might become frustrated with us like all teenagers, she'd weigh that against what she might have had and give us a break.

12

Olivia When Briony came through the front door after work, I knew something was wrong. M was better at hiding her emotions, but Briony looked stressed and upset. Based on the look she was giving me, I knew it was about me. I wanted to run upstairs to my room so that whatever they had to tell me, they couldn't say. Why did Caleb have to be spending the night at Hank's? Maybe the news wouldn't be so bad if he was here.

"Hey, Livy," Briony greeted me with a hug. "How was your last day of school?"

It had been such a good day. No more sixth grade. No more Krystal and her minions relentlessly hounding me. Next year, I'd get to switch classes every hour, and there was no way Krystal would be in every one. Eden and I celebrated that fact all day today.

"It was okay," I offered, crossing my fingers that my teacher hadn't called to say I should be held back. I did much better this year, but maybe I hadn't passed my reading comprehension test yesterday.

"Bet you're glad to be done." M was forcing her smile.

My throat got too dry to swallow. I wanted to hide. They never acted like this. I didn't think they'd be so disappointed in me that they'd ask me to leave if I got an F in something, but maybe I was wrong. Or maybe they decided that they wanted to go visit Briony's family in Vermont for the summer and couldn't get permission to take me with them. My social worker might have said okay for a two week trip. She liked Briony and M, but anything more than that would make her place me in a temporary foster home. It wouldn't be fun, but as long as I got to come back when they returned from vacation I could put up with any home.

"We have some news, sweetie," Briony finally said. She grasped my hand and pulled me down to sit next to her on the couch. Her arm came around my shoulder as M took the chair beside us. They both looked like someone had punched them.

I felt like I might barf. My eyes went back and forth between them. They could probably see that I didn't want them to say whatever they were going to say, but it wouldn't stop them from saying it.

"You're sending me to another family," I guessed quietly. I couldn't even sound hopeful that it might be a temporary move. Tears started to build in my eyes. I didn't want to leave them. I hadn't really cared the last time a family gave me this news, but I didn't like them anywhere near as much as I liked Briony and M. No, I loved Briony and M and didn't want to leave them.

"We'd never send you away." M reached for my hand.

They weren't sending me away? I was wrong? "I don't have to leave here?"

M flinched and looked away. "We would never ask you to leave."

Isn't that what we both said? If they're not asking me to leave, then I don't have to leave. So why did they look so upset?

Briony squeezed me against her. Her whole frame shuddered with the breath she took. "You remember your aunt, Nell?"

I flashed on a young woman with light brown hair and brown eyes like mine and my mom's. I nodded. "She's my mom's younger sister."

We never saw her much because she lived with my mom's parents, and they didn't talk to my mom. She'd always been nice to me, but she'd had to sneak out of the house to see us until she went off to college. When my mom died, I thought she'd come get me. She didn't. My social worker said that my aunt and my grandparents couldn't take me. Since I'd never met my grandparents, I wasn't surprised. They'd kicked my mom out of their house when she wouldn't agree to give me up for adoption. I was glad I didn't have to live with them. The guy who was my biological father wanted nothing to do with my mom when she got pregnant. He gave up his parental rights as soon as I was born. I've never met him, but I liked Aunt Nell and she knew me. I thought she'd help me. I thought she'd want me.

"She petitioned the court for custody," Briony said softly.

I shook my head totally confused. "But she didn't want me. My social worker asked her, and she didn't want me."

M knelt on the floor in front of me and reached for my other hand. "Honey, she was in college when your mom died. She probably didn't feel like she could take care of you then, but she does now. She definitely wants you."

"Did you talk to her?" Maybe they could talk her out of it.

"Your social worker called us last night," Briony told me.

"We would have told you, but we wanted to talk to Lauren first," M added.

Why would they talk to Lauren first before telling me? They probably just wanted me to get through my last day of school. That was actually nice of them.

"It sounds like your aunt has really missed you and wants you to live with her," Briony said in her everything-is-fine voice.

"Why now?"

They looked at each other. Briony's eyes started to shimmer, so M spoke up. "She's done with college. She has a good job and is about to get married. I think she's really ready for a family. I know it's confusing, but when someone's in college, that's all they can think about. Raising a niece was probably too much real life for her at a time when all she could think about was passing her classes."

"But now she's ready, and she's really excited to see you again," Briony added in a fake enthusiastic tone. "I bet she's missed your mom almost as much as you have."

How could she? She barely spent any time with us. Almost three years later, she hadn't called once and suddenly she wants me? Just when I've found the best place to live with people that I loved. I loved them. I didn't just like them. Why did I have to leave when I finally started to feel like I really belonged somewhere? When I felt like I had real parents again? This was so unfair.

"Can you try to give her a chance, Olivia?" M asked.

I wanted to cry. For days and days and never stop, like when my mom died. I didn't want to leave here, but they were saying I had to. Maybe if I asked I wouldn't have to go. I never asked for anything. It might work if I asked just this once. "Can't I stay here? Please? I'll be really good. I'll do more chores, and I'll study really hard so I won't have to bother you for homework help anymore. I'll get a job to help pay for things. Please? I don't want to leave. I want to stay here with you."

Briony let out a sob and tears poured out of her eyes. M tipped up and pulled me into a hug. She trembled and her voice sounded thick. "Honey, we want you to stay. We want that more than anything, but Lauren told us the law on this. We can't keep you if your aunt wants you. We would never ask you to leave, but we can't keep you."

I couldn't stay because my aunt, a person I barely know, wants me now. When I had foster parents who wanted to keep me for maybe another whole year, someone comes along and takes me away. This wasn't fair. My mom dying wasn't fair. Being tossed from home to home wasn't fair. The only fair thing to happen to me in three years was now being yanked away from me.

"We don't want you to go. We want you to stay. If we could fight this legally, we would. Do you understand that?" M whispered next to my ear.

My eyes filled with tears. I nodded and hugged her tight then pushed away and ran up to my room. They couldn't do anything to change this, and I didn't want them to feel worse than they already seemed to.

I flopped onto my bed and cried for a really long time. So long I felt tired afterward. My whole body ached, but I slid off the bed and went to my closet. It wasn't like I really wanted to pack, but I had to. Looking up, I remembered that I'd need to drag my chair over to the closet to reach my duffle bag. I started pulling out the clothes I remembered bringing. The social worker could show up at any time and I had to be ready. I hoped it wouldn't be till tomorrow so I could say goodbye to Caleb.

"Olivia?" M's voice came through the door as she knocked lightly. This was the only foster home where the parents knocked on the door before coming inside.

I swiped my sleeve under my nose and rubbed my face. "Come in."

The door opened and M looked inside. Her eyes landed on my clothes. They widened. "You're not leaving tonight, sweetie. I'm so sorry. We should have told you that."

"Oh." I looked at my clothes then turned and sat on my bed. "When?"

"A judge decides on Monday, but we're not sure of your aunt's timeline. We've asked your social worker to arrange a meeting, but we haven't heard back on that. We'll tell you as soon as we know."

"Monday, probably?"

"It's possible."

I nodded and started folding my clothes to place in the duffle. They'd have to come off my bed before I could sleep anyway.

M looked like she couldn't decide if she should help me. "Your clothes won't fit in your duffle anymore. We could get you a nice suitcase with wheels tomorrow if you want."

I shook my head. They shouldn't have to spend any money on me now. "They fit before."

"But you have more clothes now."

I looked up at her. She had brown eyes just like me and my mom. Sometimes I could see my mom in those eyes. "Those clothes aren't mine. If you get another foster kid, you'll need them."

She brought her hand up and gripped my chin. "Those are your clothes, Olivia. They're yours. We would have gotten you more if you'd let us. I'll help you pack, but not because I want you to leave. We want you to stay for as long as you want to stay with us. But I have to believe that living with your mom's sister is going to be good for you. I bet you'll get used to living with her in no time and you'll love it as much as I hope you love living here."

No way that would happen, but she was trying to make this okay for me. I wanted to believe her. "Okay."

She brought my duffle down from the top rack and grabbed the clothes I thought I should leave behind from the hangers. I was glad to be able to take them because I couldn't fit into some of my old clothes anymore. We began folding some things and making room in my duffle for them. It didn't take long. She was good at packing. All that hung in my closet now were the things I'd wear for the next couple of days.

"Come downstairs. We'll stay up past bedtime and watch movies together. I bet Briony is thinking of popcorn right now."

"That's okay. You go ahead." I should get used to not being with them as soon as possible.

She bent to look me in the eyes, her expression as sad as mine but very determined. "There's nothing left for you to do to get ready. Put that behind you now and come enjoy the rest of the night with us." She pulled on my arm and smiled.

I didn't know how she knew so much about how a foster kid felt, but sometimes it was like she could read my mind. I bet she even knew that I'd take being put on punishment every day if only I could stay here.

13

Olivia

On Sunday morning, I was heading downstairs when I heard Caleb raise his voice from the living room. I halted on the steps as Briony was telling him to calm down. I was pretty sure they were talking about me.

"But why?" he said. "She shouldn't have to leave. She lives here. She's ours."

"I know it feels like that, and we wish it were true," Briony told him in her best mom voice.

"Can't we adopt her? You had to do that with me. Why can't we do that with her?"

That would be so great, but it wasn't going to happen. The older girls in the group home said nobody gets adopted once they hit double digits. Parents want to adopt babies and toddlers so they get to shape how they turn out.

"Sweetie, you were different," Briony told him what I already knew. Yeah, he was different. He was her son from the beginning. "Mommy gave birth to you, and the courts let me adopt you because she and I were married. Olivia's aunt wants her. Wouldn't you want to live with Aunt Sadie or Aunt Danica if something happened to me?"

He was quiet for a long time. I didn't want to think about something happening to Briony and she wasn't even my mom. "I guess, but it really blows. Why'd they let us have her if her family could take her?"

Yeah, why? Why'd my aunt decide now to take me? Why not last summer when the other family thought I was stupid and didn't want me anymore?

"It's complicated, honey." That was every adult's way of saying that things just suck sometimes.

"Caleb," M spoke up. She didn't usually go for the things-just-suck explanation. "Her aunt was really upset when her sister died. She probably felt too sad to try to raise her sister's child when she was barely an adult herself. I know it hurts, but we can't let our wishes keep Olivia from discovering her family. That wouldn't be fair."

He didn't respond. I wouldn't have known what to say either. I decided that I should make noise on the way downstairs so they'd stop talking about me. I didn't want to spend the whole day sad when nothing could be done to change anything. Aunt Nell was coming for me and I just had to deal with it.

"Morning, Livy." Briony pulled me into a hug. I was really going to miss these. I wrapped my arms around her back and just breathed in her scent. I wanted to remember how this felt forever.

"What do you feel like for breakfast?" M asked, reaching out to stroke my shoulder.

"Waffles," Caleb whispered from beside me and pulled on my arm to get us moving toward the kitchen.

"Waffles," I echoed.

Briony laughed and kissed our foreheads. "I'll need helpers."

Caleb and I headed into the kitchen to start pulling out ingredients and mixing bowls. Briony got the waffle maker as M set the table. I could tell they were going to make my last day with them the best it could be.

"What should we do today? Something with Eden and Hank, maybe?" Briony asked me.

I looked up, happy that I'd get the chance to see them both before I had to leave. I should have known they'd think of that for me.

"A picnic?" M suggested. "Soccer in the park? A game of kickball? Rollerblading? Whatever you want to do, sweetie."

"All of it," Caleb joked.

Yeah, all of it. I only wish we had the time.

14

Olivia Shiny new cellphone in hand, I climbed out of Aunt Nell's car. We were in the parking lot of a townhouse complex. It had taken more than two hours to get here. Aunt Nell had babbled on about a lot of stuff, but I didn't really pay attention. My throat still felt like I couldn't swallow whatever was lodged in it. I hated saying goodbye to Briony, M, and Caleb this afternoon. They kept saying that I could call anytime. That they'd visit, but after that long drive, I didn't think I'd ever see them again.

We were in Maryland now, a long way from Charlottesville. Too long for them to just pop over for a visit. At least Aunt Nell seemed friendly. She was different from what I remembered. After what M had said, I guess I didn't realize that she was only twelve years older than me. She was a lot more serious now. And she looked like my mom. That was really hard. She hadn't before, but now she kinda did.

"Home sweet home." She gestured to the townhouse with the blue door.

She went around to the trunk and pulled out my stuffed duffle. I grabbed my equally stuffed backpack. Briony and M's friends had given me an eReader as a going away present. It was super nice of them. Briony and M got me a gift card so I could download as many books as I could ever read and more. Willa and Quinn gave me the phone so I could stay in touch. Willa said she wanted to get texts from me. She already paid for the service contract so I had no choice but to take it. I should have given it back because it was too expensive. But I knew I'd be desperate to text and call Eden and Caleb whenever I could and call or text Briony and M and Willa for a long as they wanted to keep talking to me.

"Let's go, Livy, I'm sure Ian is waiting for us."

Ian. Aunt Nell's fiancé. They lived together. He was a pastor and they were getting married next month. I was supposed to be in the wedding. She talked and talked and talked about the wedding plans. It took almost the entire trip here.

I followed her inside and wanted to turn around again. Stuffy, like no one ever opened the windows, and cramped compared to Briony and M's house.

"I hope he likes you," Aunt Nell said in a quiet voice.

I glanced up at her. She looked like she hadn't meant to say that to me. Yeah, me too.

"Hello, my sugarplum," a deep voice called out. A man appeared at the end of the hallway. He was tall. Not quite as tall as Jessie but pretty tall. He had a full beard and wore glasses. Some of his hair was already grey. I wondered how old he was. He must be a lot older than Aunt Nell if he was getting grey hair.

"Hi, baby." Aunt Nell dropped my duffle and raced to him for a hug and kiss. It lasted really long and made me queasy. Briony and M would never make out like this in front of me or Caleb. I'm sure they made out. They just didn't do it in front of people.

"I see you've finally got your niece." He looked over her shoulder at me. "Olivia, I'm glad to have you in my home."

His home? I thought they lived here together? "Thanks." I said because I couldn't think of what else to say.

"Isn't it wonderful, Ian? Now we can finally be a family just like you said." Aunt Nell seemed to get more serious as she talked to him. Not at all like the woman who used to come visit my mom and me.

"As it should be. No one should be raised in that way," Ian told her. He came closer and held out his arms. I didn't want to hug him, but it didn't look like I had a choice. Thankfully it didn't last long. He smelled like the storage locker filled with Caleb's baseball equipment. His clothes were clean, just stale, like this house.

"Thank you for having me." I said that to every foster family that took me in. I knew this was different, but it didn't feel much different.

"Very polite. Good. At least they didn't screw that up."

"Ian," Aunt Nell warned in a firm tone.

"What? You never know with those people."

I wasn't sure if he was talking about Briony and M or all foster parents. If he meant Briony and M, I didn't like what he was saying. He didn't know that theirs was the only house that never felt like a foster home to me.

"Let's let her get settled in."

He bent to pick up my bag and led the way up the narrow staircase. He showed me the bathroom as we passed it. We'd be sharing it. That was going to be weird. Caleb and I had to share, but our bathroom had two sinks and the shower and toilet were in a separate area with a door between. I'd get up to take a shower first and could dry my hair and brush my teeth while Caleb took his shower in private. I'd just have to learn a new routine here. It was the same at every house.

He showed me to a bedroom at the end of the hall. There was a daybed lined against one wall and a big L-shaped desk took up the rest of the room. A desktop computer with one of those old monitors covered a quarter of the desk. I felt like I'd walked into a museum display of a room from before I was born.

"Ian bought you the bed, Livy. Wasn't that nice of him? Before it was just his office." Aunt Nell's brow rose in expectation.

Before I could thank him, Ian interrupted, "I'll still need to do some work in here, but I'll knock before I come in."

This wouldn't be the first time I had to share a room, but it would be the first time I shared it with an adult. That was even worse than the bathroom arrangement. I swallowed the heavy lump again. This time it wasn't sadness at leaving Briony and M. This time it was because everything changed the moment I walked through that door, and for the first time, I didn't feel grateful that I wasn't in the group home.

I nodded and let him take my bag to the closet. When he opened it I saw that it was packed to the gills. I wouldn't be able to hang any of my clothes. I might not even be able to fit my duffle on the ground. I wish I could stop comparing things to how it was at Briony and M's. I should be happy that my mom's sister finally wanted me. Maybe we could talk about her more. Maybe we could remember the times we spent together. Maybe that would make this easier.

"We'll let you get settled in. Dinner is in two hours," Ian said and reached for Aunt Nell's hand to pull her from the room with him.

I almost started crying when he closed the door behind them. I was pretty sure that meant that I couldn't bother them until dinner two hours from now. Not that I felt like leaving the room, but it was different from being able to leave the room if I wanted.

Everything was different now. The sooner I accepted that, the easier this would be.

15

MSilence never seemed so loud. I used to welcome it, used to crave it. In this house, it meant something was off. I never thought I'd get used to voices or laughter or the noise of everyday happenings at home. Never wanted it. Now I missed it.

I set my cereal bowl in the dishwasher and glanced out at the empty living room. Briony was at a meeting with the dean. Caleb was at soccer day camp, dropped off by his mom. And Olivia was gone. Taken from us.

Pain squeezed my heart. I did this to myself. To my family. Brought in someone to love and laugh with, knowing full well that something like this could happen. It was a stupid move on my part. To think I could make up for my past, honor Kathryn with this one child. I thought I could care for her, give her a safe place to live, a loving home but know in my heart and mind that she wasn't ours. Instead I grew to love her, and I'd forced it on my family, too. It was unforgivable.

Loading everyone's dishes into the dishwasher, I shook off the melancholy. Nothing could be done to fix this situation. If I really wanted to do something, I'd tell child services that we were ready for another foster child, but I couldn't. And I wouldn't do that to Briony or Caleb. They were already upset enough, angry even. At me. They didn't realize it, but they were angry with me for suggesting this. It didn't matter that we were careful to choose a child who didn't have parents, who had family that had refused to take her in. I thought we were safe from this very thing. I'd been wrong.

But it wouldn't get any easier if I continued to dwell on it. Hopefully time would make this easier.

I left for campus at exactly the same time as yesterday. I still had my precisions that I couldn't give up, no matter how much having a family sometimes impinged on that. Caleb wasn't exactly precise, but a countdown clock helped the morning routine. He preferred an impersonal timer that looked like it came from one of his favorite action movies over his mom and me yelling out reminders of how late he was going to be. Olivia never had that problem. She was like me in that regard. Like me in a lot of regards.

I drove to campus trying not to think about how quiet the house had gotten in only a week. Caleb asked to spend every night at Hank's, and Briony had been going to bed early. They were grieving and I tried not to take it personally, but I was the one to suggest we take in a foster child. Insisted almost.

As I stepped out of my car in the nearly empty parking lot, I wondered for the first time if I should have skipped this summer session. This was usually my favorite time to teach. I liked the kids, I appreciated the shorter length of the semester, and I loved the opportunity to teach with Briony. Now that things had changed at home, I wish we hadn't signed up for summer session. We should have taken a family trip somewhere to get out, get away, leave the reminder of the empty room behind us. Instead, Briony and I were teaching our combined business venture class again, and I had one other class. Even that reminded me that I'd planned for this summer to be different. Usually I taught three classes for both sessions of summer semester. This year, our classes were confined to the first session so we could spend more time with the kids this summer.

Two associate professors passed me on one of the paths through Darden. They smiled politely at me, which I was still getting used to. The time B.B.—Before Briony—maybe three professors would speak to me.

"Oh, hey, how's Briony?" another professor, in accounting I think, gave me a standard greeting in the B.T.—Briony Timeline. They all had something to ask me now.

"Good, thanks," I replied. I would ask about the woman's husband, but I knew she wasn't trying to start a conversation.

"Yo, Prof!" a student from the venture class greeted. His buddy beside him sang out, "Professor D!"

I smiled and waved. They were the reason I taught, put myself out there in a job that normally wouldn't fit my demeanor. But I loved it and my students liked me even if my colleagues still thought I was a bit freaky.

Twenty minutes until my first class. I had enough time to duck into my office and drop my bag. With few professors left on campus for the summer, the second floor of the faculty building was as quiet as the house. I didn't mind it as much here, but the quiet seemed to be taunting me today.

I placed my laptop bag on the desk, ruffling through to find today's class notes. I didn't really need them. I taught this core class every semester. It was pretty much branded into my brain.

"Hey, hon," Briony said as she slipped into my office. Our offices were a floor and a few corridors apart, so we'd often meet in one or the other to save time before classes.

My ears tingled at the sound of her voice. I smiled before I turned around. Happiness was everywhere in my life now. Even in the face of loss, I still had Briony to hold onto.

She matched my smile and leaned forward to brush her lips against mine. She'd gone to bed before me last night and left before I got up this morning. We'd been out of sync with our schedules before, but it felt more significant this time.

"You look beautiful today." My eyes drifted over her linen skirt and shapely blouse then back up to catch the quirk of her lips. She didn't need to be told she looked beautiful. My eyes would tell her, but I still liked to say it. My heart fluttered every time she told me. I was pretty sure she felt the same way. "How'd the meeting go?"

"Like every meeting with the dean, worthless and endless."

I chuckled with her. The dean of the grad school wasn't exactly known for efficiency. He could drone on and on and be convinced it was all essential.

"Probably the last year for this class, though."

My eyebrows rose as I nodded. That made sense. Funding was getting harder to justify. They'd likely want to discontinue a class that required significant startup capital from its investment pool.

"I'll miss it." A fond smile graced my lips. I had this class to thank for my life now. My full, rich life filled with love and laughter.

"Next summer, maybe we skip teaching. Take a long break," Briony echoed my earlier thoughts.

"Whatever you want," I agreed.

She shook her head and smiled. Then she let out a sigh and sadness crept into her beautiful gaze. "Don't let me break down and get Caleb a dog."

"Oh, Bri, I'm so sorry," I said again because it was my fault. She never would have agreed to foster a child if I hadn't talked her into it.

"Stop it, M." Her hands came up to grip my face. "It's not your fault. It's sad and awful. I hate that I loved her and lost her and that you and Caleb had to go through it, but we had a wonderful family and we still do."

I pushed back the tears I felt welling in my eyes and reached for a hug. Briony's hugs could fend off all sorts of horrors.

"Don't let Caleb guilt me into a dog," she sighed and clutched me tighter.

"I'll see if Willa will let us dog-sit for a while. That'll make him happy."

She pulled back and smiled, some of the sadness gone from her expression. "You always have good ideas."

"Ladies," Javier stepped into the doorway as he did on occasion, even when Briony wasn't here. His office was six doors down, and he always made a point of greeting me each day. "How's tricks?"

"Javi!" Briony's tone showed her surprise. "What are you doing here?" Her eyes darted to me, checking as she always did on my comfort level. Other than students, I rarely let anyone into my office. But Javier and Alexa didn't exactly do boundaries. It was that callous disregard that actually made me moderately comfortable with them.

"Stopped by to walk with your woman over to our classes. Didn't expect to find you here."

Briony's grin flashed bright. She flicked her eyes to me, pride and happiness shining through. She always relaxed when she detected my ease in social situations.

"How's my boy?" Javier asked about Caleb. He'd been his soccer coach for three years now and really cared for him. He also came in handy as an everyday male role model when Caleb's grandfathers were in another state.

"Better," Briony answered truthfully. "Still acting up a bit." Or a lot, but we expected that to settle down as soon as he got into a regular summer routine.

"That camp doesn't tire him out every day?" Javier's dark eyebrows slanted down in a frown. He wasn't able to fit in being the assistant coach this year and looked guilty about it.

"Not enough, apparently. I was thinking of letting him be Quinn's ball boy at her basketball camp this summer."

"That might do it. Or you could just give him to Jessie for a week. He'd be so tired he wouldn't even have thoughts of angst."

We chuckled. We'd already come up with a reason for him to spend a day with Jessie. The effect lasted a couple of days, but then he got snippy about something again and took it out on his mom. It was all a way to cover his hurt, along with some new teenage hormones.

We'd just have to be more creative and attentive. I wasn't going to let this sadness become a permanent fixture in my family's life. We would work at it together because that's what families did.

16

MI rapped my knuckles on Willa's office doorframe. She looked up and smiled, undisturbed by my drop-in. I almost always called, but I was still out of sorts these days.

"Hey, M. Glad you're here. I could use the break." She leaned back in her chair and watched as I took a seat across from her desk.

"Hi. Hope I'm not interrupting anything."

She shook her head. The dark brown waves in her hair were more curly than wavy today. The length had gone from shorter to medium over the years I'd known her, but the style remained the same. I liked that about her. Consistent and reliable. "How's the venture class going?"

Three weeks into the class and it was fun but bittersweet. Kinda like the summer Briony and I were having. "It's good this year. Only two businesses, but the kids are getting more and more creative each year."

"As long as none of them are starting gaming companies, I'm all for it."

I laughed. Willa could always make me laugh.

Her eyes darted away. "Have you heard from her?"

My breath deserted me. One thing about Willa, she knew me pretty well. It scared me sometimes. "Last Sunday. She said everything was okay, but she sounded so, I don't know...small."

Her eyes came back to mine. "Like she wasn't happy?"

"Like she did when we had to tell her that her aunt was going to take her from us."

"Really sad still?"

"Yes." I didn't want to admit it, but I'd heard it in her voice. She was trying to be brave, and so were we, but we were all sad.

"You're worried?"

I couldn't really voice what I was feeling. Yes, worried, sad, angry, anxious, almost like I had the first time I walked into a foster home. I didn't know what to expect, if it would be good or bad. I was worried for her for more reasons than I wanted to admit.

Willa pulled open a desk drawer. She brought up a file folder and handed it to me. "You're probably going to get really upset with me for this, but I can be an asshole and everyone knows that about me."

I couldn't imagine what she'd have in there that would upset me. She thought she wasn't the best person in our group. She could be grumpy and short tempered, but she was never an asshole. Definitely never to me.

Opening the file, I glanced down at the top page. The subject line was Ian Corcoran. I looked up at Willa, my mouth open and my heart pounding. She'd run a background check on Olivia's aunt's boyfriend. I didn't know what to feel about this. I should be upset that she'd been so presumptuous, so overbearing as to take on a responsibility that wasn't hers, but instead, I think I felt grateful. I'd been worried when I found out Nell was living with a man. I didn't want to think that anything bad could happen to Olivia, but it kept me from sleeping well most nights.

The report told me that he was a thirty-nine-year-old pastor born in Silver Spring, Maryland. He'd been leading his own church for eleven years. Four former addresses showed up on the page along with his current residence, which he owned. He'd never been married and volunteered at the food kitchen attached to his church. He had no felonies, misdemeanors, or arrests. Blank spaces after words like "Day 1"were listed along with words like "Time and Location." It was an incomplete report, which made me both glad and anxious.

I caught Willa's nervous look. Yeah, she should be nervous. This was a complete overreach on her part. Panic slammed into me. What if she'd done this to me? As soon as the panic started, I quashed it. She wouldn't do that to me, her friend. She just wouldn't. "Why did you do this?"

"Everything in there comes from public records. We have a firm that runs background checks on all potential hires to avoid some of the mistakes we made at first."

That didn't explain why she would do this. "But what would make you run a background check on him?"

"There's one on her, too."

I looked back down at the file and flipped to another page. Nell looked good on paper, too. It made me feel better. A lot better, especially since I hadn't done it. I would have felt guilty if I'd initiated a search like this. I'd felt uncomfortable even running a browser search for her name when the social worker first told us about her. Other than a typically boring Facebook page, nothing seemed concerning. I looked up at Willa again.

"She's your kid, M. You can't make it legal, but she's yours. I didn't want you to worry that anything would happen to her."

I cleared my throat. "You did this for me?"

"Of course." She frowned at my question. "I can get our investigators to do a more extensive check if you want. I've had to learn the hard way that one week of twenty-four hour surveillance can save a lot of headaches."

I stared at her, trying to figure out why she'd do something like this. Overstep like this. My head shook at her suggestion. As much as I wanted to know if this Ian guy was bad news, I couldn't justify invading someone's privacy for my curiosity and peace of mind. I had to have faith that Nell wouldn't choose a pervert to marry.

"You're shocked."

I was. She'd always treated me differently from others in her group of friends. It was subtle, and I thought it was because I was so different from them. Everyone in the group had somehow benefited from her wealth. They were all grateful, certainly, but she'd shared her wealth from this successful software company with them like they were her dependents. She'd never offered to buy anything for me, and I'd always been grateful for that. I wouldn't know how to turn her down without insulting her.

"Not that I did this," she was saying. "You're shocked that I'd do this for you."

Jeez, she really did know me well.

"I'm going to say this once and in a way that I know only you will understand." Her eyes locked on mine, something she rarely did.

I waited, a little panicked that she might express a sentiment that I couldn't reciprocate.

"You're my phone call."

My eyes flitted away, down to my hands, and back up to meet hers. I wasn't sure which phone call she meant.

She let out a breath of air and broke eye contact. "If I ever did something bad, like really bad, you'd be my phone call."

I pushed out the breath I was holding. I could think of several bad things I could do. Not the kind of bad things someone in our group would think of, like getting a DUI. That would be bad, but not the kind of bad I could dream up. My kind of bad could be seen as malicious, even if I were protecting myself. The kind of bad things I'd envisioned doing to some men prior to meeting Briony.

Yes, that was it. The difference that I recognized in Willa, the reason why she and I meshed as friends so well. She could do those bad things, too.

"Quinn would still love me," she continued. "She'd try to understand why I did what I did. She'd stand by me, but she'd never think of me the same way. It would ruin her." She shrugged and glanced back at me. "So if I needed someone to think through all of my options after doing something bad, you'd be the call."

Talk about an eye opening conversation. "Okay." Seemed a stupid thing to say, but that was how easy it was to accept. Because I knew she was right. Briony was a lot darker than Quinn. She could deal with anything bad I might do. If Willa ever did anything bad, I'd want to be there to help her figure out what to do about it.

"Okay," she agreed.

I took a breath and plowed ahead with something I would never have asked her before. "Can I ask you something?"

She smiled briefly and nodded.

"Why haven't you ever tried to make me take some of your money?" Immediately, I realized that sounded off. "Everything you did for your friends. You've pretty much financed their dreams."

She flushed red and looked away, her head shaking as if to deny what I'd said. "I guess I thought you might consider it insulting."

Not insulting, but definitely not how I'd like a real friendship to be. But there had always been one weakness for me prior to meeting Briony, and she had to know it. "Not even for a cochlear implant for Hank?"

Her eyes pinged back to mine, widening in surprise. "I'm sorry. I just assumed that he wanted to be deaf. If that's not the case, you don't even need to ask."

I waved her off before she said any more. My heart filled with pride for her. "No, that's exactly right. There's nothing wrong with being deaf. Few hearing people understand that. I should have known you'd get it."

"Good, okay, then. But it should go without saying, if you ever need anything that I can do, just say it."

My eyes grew moist. I couldn't stop it. "That's...that's..."

"Just so we're clear." She saved me from having to voice my emotions. "And I know I overstepped here, but I liked that kid so much. I want her to be safe. I want you to know she's safe."

"You didn't have him followed and not tell me about it, did you?"

Her lips twitched. "No, but one phone call and it'll be done."

"No. Thank you, though. This makes me feel better about it."

Her smile faded. "I'm sorry you lost her."

I nodded crisply. I was sorry, too. But I also tried to be happy for Olivia. If Kathryn had a sister, I would have wanted to know her.

"You're an amazing woman, M. I don't have the courage to take in a child and raise her, provide a safe place for her. You did it so well."

I shook off her compliment. "You could do it. Anyone could."

"Anyone should, but not everyone can."

I pushed the file folder back to her. She took it without question and returned it to her desk drawer. Anyone else probably would have insisted I take it with me. "I'm glad I stopped by."

She smiled. "Me, too."

17

For the second time this week, I nearly fell on my face as soon as I walked through my front door. Damn! It! Both Caleb and Briony's shoes were right in the path of the front door like miniature stable jumps for anyone coming inside. Problem was, no one ever looked down when they first walked in the door. And I'd told them this, many, many times.

I always knew that no one would be as neat as I was. No one as ordered. I made allowances for that when I readied myself to live with Briony and her son. I had to come to grips with the fact that I would do more cleaning because I liked things much neater than, well, any human I'd ever met. I accepted that truth. For Briony's love, it wasn't even a factor. Still, the reality of it, sometimes daily, could grate on my nerves. Especially after a long day at work.

Taking a deep breath, I nudged the shoes out of the way, lining them up against the foyer wall where they'd forgotten to place them. Where they knew I liked the shoes to be placed if they were going to take them off as soon as they got home. Living with someone, no matter how much I loved her and how wonderful her child was, turned out to be harder than anything I'd done in my adult life. It was also more wonderful than anything I'd experienced in my adult life. But on days like today when I was hot and tired and still filled with sorrow, trip hazards as soon as I entered my very own sanctuary stirred my blood to a low boil.

"Why not?" Caleb's raised voice hit me from the living room as I kicked off my dress shoes, placed them against the wall, and stepped into the comfy sneakers I wore in the house. "Everyone else has one."

"Because you don't need one. We said when you got to high school. We agreed on that."

"You agreed to that," he snapped, very un-Caleb-like, making me halt my progress down the hallway.

I could hear Briony's sigh from twenty feet away. "Ninth grade, Caleb. That's it."

"I'm the only dweeb at camp who doesn't have one. I'll be the only dweeb in eighth grade without one. Even Olivia got one before she left. How come it's okay that she has one but I don't?"

"One, we didn't get it for her, Willa did. And two, it was the only way to ensure we could all stay in touch with her. Unlike your situation, she actually needed one."

"I can't even text her." The anguish in his voice lathered me in guilt.

"You can use your very handy iPad, which you begged me to get you last summer because you were the only dweeb at camp without one of those if I recall. I'm pretty sure you can text her and any of your other non-dweeb friends at camp or school on that. No one will know you don't have a phone."

"Everyone will know!" he practically screeched, sounding more like a variety of bird than a teenage boy. "Come on, Mom. It's only a year early."

"We'll see," she said, which meant she'd think of some other argument for saying no tomorrow.

"That always means no," her very astute son told her.

"You're right," Briony's weary voice caused a twinge in my heart. She must have had a hard day, too. "Last day of summer next year, you can pick the phone you want."

"That doesn't help me now."

"Nope."

"This sucks!" he griped.

"I'm sure it does," his mom agreed. She must be too tired to remind him of his tone. For the three years I'd been a part of this family, I could count on one hand the number of times Caleb acted up like this. He was pretty even keeled, almost always cheery. Sure, he'd hit his teenage years, but until this summer, those expected angry teen moments hadn't yet surfaced.

"I want to spend the night at Hank's."

"Not tonight," Briony told him.

"Why not?" This seemed to be a favorite of his now.

"Because you've spent the last four nights at his house. You've overstayed your welcome."

"He wants me there."

"It matters what his grandmother wants."

"She likes me."

"I know she does, but that doesn't mean she wants to raise you. We're going to give her a break for a while. You can spend the night in your very own room filled with all those other things you were convinced would make you lame if you didn't have them."

"Man!" He said it like he was swearing up a storm. "You don't let me do anything. I hate it here. There's nothing to do. No one to hang out with. You're trying to ruin my life!"

With that declaration, I heard slapping feet on our refinished original hardwoods as he ran down the hallway, barely registering that I was standing in his path before swooping around me and pounding up the staircase. Three-two-one, SLAM! His door frame was probably hanging in shreds with the power of that door slam.

Briony's head was bent when I joined her in the living room. I stepped up behind her and slid my arms around her middle, resting my chin on her shoulder. "Tough day?"

She shook her head and sighed, leaning back against me. "I should just get him the phone. He's gotten so…so…I don't know. Just a few weeks ago, he was a sweet kid. How could it go so wrong so quickly?"

"Demon possession?"

She laughed and the tightness in my chest loosened. My hard day suddenly forgotten. Her happiness was my quest. For someone who used to spend much of her time living inside herself, having a quest like this helped.

"You're not getting him a phone or a dog. You don't want or like either. You said ninth grade, he understands that. He doesn't like it, but he understands it. You start switching the rules now and he'll smell the blood in the water. He'll circle you with his fin up for every moment of his high school years. Stay firm, my sweet."

Her golden eyes softened. "I love you, you know? You're exactly what I need. What we need."

I slid my hand down her arm to her hand, fingering her engagement ring. The one I had inscribed with the very sentiment she just voiced. It was my way of telling her I loved her when I still had trouble saying the words. "You're all I'll ever need."

She turned in my arms and kissed me, taking her time to show me how much she loved me. When she pulled back we were both breathless. "How was your afternoon class?"

"Fine," I said automatically because really, what were entitled-acting college students compared to a stepson who was hurting so much he was lashing out at his once adored mother?

"Any requests for dinner?" She brushed her fingers through my hair as her other hand stroked patterns over my chest. It still amazed me how easy this was for me now. How much having her this close made everything in my life good.

"Caleb's favorite."

She flashed a bright smile. "Now who's bribing him?"

"It's not a bribe so much as a project." I watched her head tilt in interest as I started backing down the hall. "We'll see if it works."

Upstairs Olivia's door stood open. I'd closed it just yesterday, which meant that either Briony or more likely Caleb had opened it to look inside. It might have been the instigator for this mini-fit of his.

I knocked twice on Caleb's closed door. No immediate response, so I rapped again. Harder.

"What?" he bellowed from inside.

I eased the door open. "Hi."

His face registered shock, regret, then annoyance once again. He just looked at me, but I held firm until he finally relented. "Hey, M."

I came in and gestured to the edge of his bed, asking if I could sit. He never minded before. In fact, he was more of a door's always open kinda person. We'd had to train him to knock on all closed doors.

He gave me a shrug but watched as I took the seat, careful not to crowd his legs that seemed to be getting longer by the minute. His clothes from camp that day were strewn haphazardly near his closet. He must have tossed them toward the hamper and not cared if they made it in or not. It was fine with me as long as his room didn't start to smell from the unwashed clothes or any food he smuggled up here. Briony was more of a stickler about him cleaning his room.

"I caught most of that as I came in, big guy," I started, trying not to sound like a scolding parental unit and more like a concerned confidante. "I know you're sometimes angry. I know the feeling can just creep up on you. It's easy to vent to the people you know won't hold it against you."

"She holds everything against me."

"You know that's not true." I stared him down until he jerked his chin in agreement. "And I know you miss Olivia. We all do. That anger you feel, it's really just you hurting."

He looked away then whipped his legs off the bed and lurched over to his beanbag chair. Every bone in his body collapsed in on themselves as he dropped into the cushy seat. "It sucks."

"Yeah, it does. It wasn't fair. It wasn't a good thing for us. It hurts like crazy. But we can't get mad at each other, Caleb. We can't let that sadness make us hurt others."

His eyes welled up, and he swallowed hard. "I just get so..."

"I know. I heard a girl laugh on campus today, and I could have sworn it was Olivia. It just made the hurt hurt more, you know?"

"Yeah."

"Your mom loves you more than anything in the world. She's hurting, too. She doesn't deserve to be yelled at."

"I didn't yell," he mumbled, but he looked sufficiently guilty.

"Okay, she doesn't deserve to have her kid, the person she loves more than life itself, tell her that she's ruining his life. Don't ya think?" My eyebrows rose and accompanied a teasing smile. "Maybe you were a little hard on her?"

"Yeah. But I am the only kid without a cellphone. Hank got one yesterday."

Ah, there it was. Hank got one, so Caleb would want one. "You know that the texting function on a cellphone will help Hank communicate with people who don't always understand him when he speaks. He actually needs a phone and you just want one."

"Yeah, yeah."

"Face it, you've got a mom who thinks cellphones are causing the downfall of civility. Consider yourself lucky that she's even letting you get one next year."

His lips pulled wide. "Hank said I could use his anytime I wanted."

"Brilliant. You've already got a temporary solution. Now all that's left..."

He looked expectantly at me.

"Is to..." I went on.

He still gave me a blank look.

"Apologize for being a clone of Damien, maybe?"

He laughed, not that he'd seen the movie, but some of his friends had seen the remake so he knew the reference. "Yeah, okay."

"Now, bucko," I used his mom's favorite pet name for him. "It's taco night, and you're the only one who can chop the onions without crying."

He laughed again, that sweet boy I'd first met at Hank's house and later gotten to know and love always seemed to win out, even when he was being his most demonic.

18

MLaughter erupted from the sofa cluster. I glanced over from the dining table not at all surprised to see Willa leaving the group on her way over to me. She was a master at drive-by entertainment. Stop off to hear a topic, drop an amusing line or two on the subject, and whisk herself away before the topic becomes stale.

"What are you doing?"

"Setting the table," I said as I did any Sunday night that we joined the friends for dinner. It kept me from having to take part in many conversations. Or having Briony or Willa help me through them.

"If you do this, how do I stay away from the annoying ones?" She smiled brightly, knowing exactly why I was doing this.

We glanced back over at the group where the most boisterous of the crowd, Des, was holding court. I'd actually gotten somewhat used to her when she was restoring the historical home Briony and I bought. She does good work, talks too much and is nosy as hell, but she does good work.

The baby started crying again. It pretty much only ever cried, or at least, that's all I ever saw it do. And yes, I should call it by its gender but so far I could only label it a crying machine. Sam and Caroline looked exhausted, acted exhausted, and used these dinners as their best chance to pass off the baby to other willing arms and zone out. I tried not to frown whenever I saw them or the baby. They'd spent hundreds of thousands to get that child, first with donor sperm then in vitro fertilization. When neither worked, they chose the more expensive option of utilizing a gestational carrier rather than a surrogate so they could use Caroline's eggs to have a biological baby. At first I felt bad that they couldn't get pregnant, but then I started thinking about all the barely year-old babies in the foster care program that could have used their love and care and not cost them a dime, or rather, cost Willa a dime.

Isabel scooped up the baby before Sam or Caroline even made a move off the couch. She beat Skye to the bassinette by five seconds. Isabel obviously missed holding babies now that her daughter was almost seventeen. Kayin, her partner, well, renewed partner after a yearlong separation, moved to the other side of the group. She clearly didn't want Isabel getting any ideas about babies.

Jessie, Lauren, and Briony all made their way outside where Quinn was grilling dinner. This had been a standard action for many of the group since the baby's arrival six months ago. All that time that Sam and Caroline were trying for a baby, I doubted they counted on having one that never stopped crying.

Willa tipped her head and smiled as she watched them sneak outside. She gestured for us to go into the kitchen so we could distance ourselves from the squalling child. "My ears!"

"Pretty loud," I agreed.

"It's like that assignment in high school where you have to take home an animated doll to prove that you can take care of a kid. Only the doll malfunctions and cries all the time and you get an F."

I laughed and gave her my best sarcasm. "Yes, it's exactly like that."

"Holy lungs," Quinn whispered when she appeared at the other end of the kitchen with Jessie, Lauren, and Briony. They must have circled the house to come back in through the front door.

"You don't have to whisper, Q," Jess told her. "Nobody can hear anything with Summer around."

Briony came over to slip her arm around my waist. I'd gotten comfortable enough at these dinners that I didn't need her near me at all times as my touchstone anymore. But damn, it still felt nice when she was.

"Austy brought earplugs last time," Lauren said. "I think I'll follow her lead next time."

"Or stay home like she did," Jessie inserted.

"How's Caleb really doing at your camp, Quinn? We barely get grunts from him these days." Briony joked, although she wasn't far off in her description. At least it was more from exhaustion than attitude this time.

"He's been a great help," Quinn replied. "He's the only help I've got that isn't trying to get a scholarship from me. I'm rethinking my hires for these camps from now on."

Briony beamed with pride. I puffed up pretty big, too. We'd been a little reticent to have Caleb work at Quinn's basketball camp because it wouldn't be anything like his work at Willa's, sitting at a table playing video games all day. He'd be outside in oppressive heat, running after balls, towels, water bottles, whatever Quinn and her assistant coaches needed. To hear he'd been doing well, treating Quinn the right way eased our minds.

I reached up to rub Briony's back. She flashed a grin at me. "I'm glad he's helpful."

"The campers love him. You're going to have a heartbreaker on your hands as soon as he starts dating girls, Bri."

She chuckled and nodded. We'd worry about that when he finally starting showing some real interest beyond crushes on girls. For now, we were working on trying to get back to normal in our house. Having a distraction like Quinn's basketball camp helped tremendously. Over the past week, our old pattern of life was starting to emerge again. Dinner together and some sort of game, board or sports in the backyard, then maybe a television show or two before we all went to bed. Happy, for the most part.

In less than a month, we'd begun to deal with our loss and make an effort at moving on. I doubted I'd ever fully accomplish that, but it was better than knowing my family was suffering daily.

19

Olivia Ian was talking to Aunt Nell about me again. About why I wasn't more talkative or why I wasn't making friends with the kids in the complex. He didn't understand that a bunch of young boys and two older girls wouldn't exactly want me around. He'd introduced me to all the kids that go to his church, but none of them lived near here. He wasn't going to drive me to their houses, so until school started, I sat in my room and practiced my reading or went for walks around the complex.

I missed hanging out with Caleb, Eden, and Hank. They could make a boring afternoon fun. I didn't want to miss them. I'd never missed anyone but my mom before, and now I was missing my friends. And I really missed Briony and M and how they'd help with homework or suggest games or activities to keep us from being bored. And I missed those wonderful Saturdays when we'd all do something special together.

My room didn't feel like my room because Ian was at the desk three or four hours a day. When he wasn't at the church, he was home. A lot more than Aunt Nell was home from her job. I stayed out of his way, in the living room, walking around outside, or helping Aunt Nell cook dinner. He spent a lot of time writing his sermons. Only a little more time than he spent reading them on Sundays. That was another difference. Most of my foster families made me go to church, but Briony and M never made me go. M went to church on some religious holidays, but she never forced us to go with her. Ian made us spend half the day on Sunday at church. We'd listen to him talk about whatever subject he wanted, lots to do with values and morals and how it was important to be part of the community. I found out that didn't always mean helping others. It meant not being different. Then we'd sit in the church basement for another couple of hours in meetings with adults about tasks and gatherings. It was hard to keep my eyes open sometimes.

When one of his sermons went on about how being gay was wrong, I wanted to scream in the middle of church. I wouldn't have liked what he said even before I'd lived with Briony and M. I'd never met anyone gay before, but my mom taught me not to be afraid of new things. I didn't know if Ian's problem was fear or if he'd had some bad experience before, but if he knew Briony and M or Willa and Quinn or Jessie and Lauren, he wouldn't be saying some of the things he said.

My shoulders slouched as I pushed up from the floor and headed to the stairs. I couldn't take them talking about me anymore, so I decided to do something I hated doing. I would lie.

"Aunt Nell?" I called out from the bottom of the staircase, giving them plenty of time to stop talking about me before I got to them. "Can I go over to the park at the end of the street? Janna invited me to play soccer with her cousins."

"Oh? Who's Janna?" Aunt Nell asked, clearly pleased.

"She knows one of the kids from this complex. They were over here yesterday." That just popped into my head.

"Sure, Livy, have fun," Aunt Nell said and smiled at Ian.

"Does she come from a good Christian family?" Ian stopped my turn to the door.

I tried not to frown. What did that mean? What was a bad Christian family? And if he ever met Eden, would I be allowed to hang out with her if he knew she was Jewish? I answered the way I thought he'd want me to. "I haven't met her parents, but she and her cousins are very nice."

"Tell them that they're always welcome at my church. Be back by seven for dinner."

"Okay," I called and dashed out the door before I had to lie even more. Hopefully they'd be content that I had a friend and wouldn't insist on knowing a lot about her. I'd have to make notes if I was going to come up with details.

Taking my time, I walked toward the park. It wasn't exactly at the end of the block. More like three blocks away, but I didn't want Aunt Nell saying I couldn't go because it was too far. When I arrived, I spotted kids playing on the swing set and elaborate fortress. Off in the distance, a softball game played on. I could watch that game for a while. Maybe I'd run around the track a few times. Caleb had been training for the track team before I left. I went running with him every once in a while. That might be fun to start again.

So far, living with Aunt Nell hadn't been the wonderful bonding over my mom experience I'd hoped it would be. She never talked about her. I showed her the memory book that M gave me. M and I had worked on filling it with the photos I had and jotting down the things I remembered about my mom. Things I never thought I'd forget like hair color, eye color, how she smelled, her favorite hobbies, but as the time passes, I've been forgetting more and more. The memory book would always be there for me to confirm the things I remembered. M could come up with a million questions to prompt memories for me to write down. When I showed the book to Aunt Nell, it just seemed to make her sad. Ian asked her once how old my mom was when she had me. The scowl on his face made it clear the subject of a sixteen-year-old mother was closed.

I wasn't too young to see how hard it was for my mom. Her parents were really upset about her getting pregnant so young. They demanded she give me up for adoption. When she didn't, they kicked her out of their house. She'd stayed with a family friend at first. Then she found another single mom to room with. Their different work schedules allowed them to switch off child care for a few years. We'd only been living on our own for three years before Mom's car accident. We didn't have much, but we didn't need much either. She tried not to be angry with her parents for kicking her out, but I think she was. She never took the anger out on Aunt Nell, though. She was always happy to see her sister whenever Aunt Nell could sneak out.

I wondered if she'd still be happy to see her now. Ian took over everything we did. He had an opinion about everything. It was always what he wanted for dinner, what he needed to do after church, what time he wanted to do the things he wanted to do. I didn't think my mom would have liked him, but she'd give him more than a month to get to know him before deciding that. I could do the same. I'd lived with foster families that I didn't like. I could live with him.

I stepped up onto the bleachers to join the people watching the softball game. My shoulders relaxed, and I felt free for the first time since moving here. No one talking about me, shushing each other because I'd come into the room, lecturing about what was right and wrong. I could just watch the game. It wouldn't be as fun as watching Hank and Caleb's baseball team, but it would be fine for now.

20

Olivia Their argument woke me up. Normally their disagreements didn't last long, and Ian always got his way. It didn't sound like that this time. They weren't discussing how much the wedding was going to cost either. It was only a week away now. They talked about it nonstop all the time. My play dates with the imaginary Janna were getting more frequent just so I could get away from them.

"How could you do this to me?" Aunt Nell demanded.

"It was a mistake, sugarplum. A slip up. The bible says, temptation—"

"I don't care what the bible says right now, Ian. You were unfaithful. We're getting married next week. How could you do this to me?"

Unfaithful. Did that mean what I thought it meant? If so I didn't think "good Christian folk" did stuff like that. Aunt Nell sounded really, really mad.

"My precious, please be reasonable. I was a fool. I will never do it again. You are the only one for me." He sounded like he was pleading now. He never pleaded. "I was under so much pressure with this wedding and raising your niece. I lost my head for a moment."

"With Angela? Why did it have to be Angela? She's going to tell everyone. It's humiliating."

"She won't say a word."

Aunt Nell didn't say anything for a while. I shouldn't be listening, but I couldn't believe they were fighting like this so close to their wedding. "I don't care, Ian. You hurt me. I can't possibly trust you now, and I can't forgive this."

"You have to, Nellie. Please. I made one mistake. God knows we're all flawed." His sermon last week was on human flaws. Totally lopsided, too. He had lots to say about women's flaws but he only made jokes about men's flaws. "You're not perfect either. We're both going through a transition right now. We've had to adjust to raising your niece. That's been hard on both of us. She's not easy. You know that."

Great. Now I was the reason he was making Aunt Nell mad? Other foster parents would fight about us kids from time to time, but this sounded like Ian blamed me for him acting badly. That being my parent, which he so wasn't, was the reason he made this kind of mistake.

"That's no excuse," Aunt Nell told him. My stomach hurt when she didn't deny his words. Parenting wasn't easy, I knew that, but she could have at least told him she liked having me here.

"I made a mistake. We love each other. We can get past this."

"I'm just so angry with you. I thought you were different from the men my age. You're a pastor and still you make this mistake. Do you know how many of my boyfriends have cheated on me?" Aunt Nell was almost screeching now. "All of them. It's why I was so open to dating you, a pastor fifteen years older. I thought you would have gotten that out of your system. You said you loved me and still you sleep with someone else. We can't get married now. Not when your secretary, the woman who has been helping us plan this wedding, was the person you slept with."

Yuck. I'd met Angela. She smoked and smelled like the three cats she had. Ian had Aunt Nell who was much younger and prettier. Why would he bother with Angela? I so didn't understand grownups.

"Sugarplum, you don't mean that. We're going to be married next week. Just please, sleep on it. I will make it up to you."

"I'm not staying here tonight. I'd go to my parents, but they won't let me in the house with Nina's kid. We'll stay at Paige's. I don't want to talk to you or see you tonight."

Ian stayed silent for a while. "Fine. I know you're angry. Take tonight. Stay with your friend. Olivia can stay here. You'll come back tomorrow, and we'll sit down when we're less emotional."

I crossed my fingers that Aunt Nell wouldn't leave me here with him. I hadn't asked her for much since coming to live with her, but I'd ask her to take me with her for sure.

"I'm just so mad at you, Ian. I can't believe you'd be like all the others."

"You know I'm not. You know this was a mistake. Take tonight. We'll talk tomorrow."

Aunt Nell didn't say anything. I stood up from my perch on the stairwell and raced back to my room so she wouldn't catch me listening. It didn't take long before she came upstairs and stopped in my doorway. "Olivia, come on. We're staying at my friend's tonight. She needs some help."

"Okay." I didn't care that she lied about why we needed to leave. I was just glad she was taking me with her without having to ask her. I grabbed my backpack and stuffed some clothes inside. I could live with this for as long as Aunt Nell needed to stay away. I felt guilty that I hoped it would be for a long time.

She went to her room and took much longer to pack than I had. I used the extra time to double check what I was taking. I wouldn't want to force her to come back here before she was ready if I forgot something.

"Let's go," she reappeared at my door. She practically flew down the stairs. It was hard to keep up with her, but at least Ian didn't try to stop us.

In the car, she didn't say anything. Her eyes were hard and filled with tears that didn't spill. I felt bad for her. She must be hurting, but I was glad that she finally stood up to Ian.

We pulled into an apartment complex. Aunt Nell spoke for the first time since we'd gotten into the car. "Paige was my college roommate. She's really nice. You'll like her."

"Okay." I reached out and squeezed her arm.

She gripped my hand, breathing in and letting it out slowly. "Let's go see her."

Paige gave Aunt Nell a hug as soon as the door opened. She smiled at me from over Aunt Nell's shoulder and welcomed me in. Her boyfriend was there, but as soon as he saw us, he kissed her goodnight and went back to his apartment. Paige showed me to her bedroom and turned on the television for me. She brought in a bunch of DVDs to select from. I felt more welcome here in two minutes than I'd felt the entire time at Ian's. She and Aunt Nell went back to the living room to talk. I was glad my aunt had someone she could talk to about this.

I settled in to watch a movie and tried not to wonder about how much my life would change again.

21

Olivia
The wedding was canceled. I was happy about that. I didn't think Ian was the right guy for Aunt Nell. Not that I'd hurt her feelings and tell her.

Three days later, Aunt Nell hadn't gotten any less angry. Thankfully, Paige seemed okay with that and having us stay here. Her place was a two bedroom, not very big, especially since Paige used the second bedroom as her office when she worked from home. They moved the desk out to the living room so that Aunt Nell could have the second bedroom. I was on the couch. It was a pullout couch, but even foster homes required that all kids get a bed. I'd never had my own room until Briony and M's, but I'd been spoiled there. Aunt Nell was too stressed to figure out what to do right now. She just knew she didn't want to move back in with Ian or marry him.

He called four or five times a day. It upset her and I wanted to tell him to stop, but it wasn't my place. Paige told him off once, which was funny to hear. Aunt Nell should talk to him like that.

Now she was worried about money. She talked to Paige about it, and sometimes it was in front of me. It made me feel guilty that she had more to worry about with me around.

"It's too bad you guys wouldn't fit here. I could use my old roommate back," Paige was saying while I started breakfast.

"We'd just get in your way. Thanks for letting us crash until I can figure something out."

Only three days had passed, but Aunt Nell already sounded younger, more like her friend Paige and less like the perfect wife Ian seemed to want her to be.

"That asshole!" Paige declared for like the twentieth time. I'd been a little intimidated by her the first few times, but now I knew she was helping Aunt Nell blow off steam.

"Why does this always happen to me?"

"Girl, you keep going for the wrong kinda man."

"I may never get the chance," Aunt Nell said and glanced at me before looking at Paige again. I wish I hadn't seen it. I was too expensive and I would make it harder for her to meet someone. For like the millionth time I silently wished she'd never come to get me. M and Briony never made me feel this way.

"Sure, you will."

"I don't want to think about that right now."

"I get you. Don't worry. Soon enough you'll be back to yourself." Paige really was a good friend to her.

"Hope so. It won't magically get us an apartment though, will it?"

"Wish you could stay here, but we've got plenty of places to look at today."

By the end of the day, we'd seen three apartments. They seemed fine, but Aunt Nell wasn't too thrilled with them. They definitely weren't as new as Paige's place, which was something they kept saying. I didn't really understand what she did for a living, something to do with people's paychecks. Whatever it was, it didn't pay enough for a place as nice as Paige's and she wasn't happy about it. I volunteered to sleep on a pullout couch if she wanted a one bedroom. I couldn't imagine spending years on a couch, but I couldn't be choosy either. I'd do whatever she needed.

When she brought up school districts, my stomach started to hurt. One of the apartments was okay, but the manager showing the unit said the middle school nearby wasn't the greatest. I doubted that my aunt thought of this when she made the decision to take me out of foster care. I wish I had the courage to tell her that she could send me back, but it was too scary to think about. There's no way I'd find another home like Briony and M's here. My only choice was to stick with my aunt and hope that I didn't become a burden.

Aunt Nell's cellphone rang. She looked at the display then at me. Before taking the call, she went into her bedroom. Paige and I looked at each other. I think we both hoped that it wasn't Ian.

Unfortunately the apartment wasn't large enough for me to miss her saying, "Hi, Mom."

I didn't know how often she spoke to her mom, but this was the first time I'd heard her. She didn't talk about her mom to me, but I was pretty sure they talked to each other. She'd invited her parents to the wedding, but her mom wasn't involved in all the planning.

Her voice got louder, enough for us to hear every word. Paige turned up the television, but it didn't stop me from hearing what she was saying.

"I can't do that, Mom. It wouldn't be right," she paused for a few seconds. "It's what I thought I had to do. What Ian wanted for us to be a family. I felt good about it." It sounded like she was telling her mom that she'd called off her wedding. Paige had made a lot of phone calls for her, helping her cancel the plans and the guests, but I hadn't heard them call her mom.

"Sure it's tough, but I don't understand why you can't just meet her. Nina made the mistake, Mom. Olivia didn't do anything wrong."

Oh, brother. It wasn't about the wedding. It was about me.

Paige gripped my arm and asked, "Want to go outside?"

I was nodding when I heard Aunt Nell say, "I need your help. I can't do this by myself."

That made me feel even worse. I'd never met my grandmother before, but I didn't like that she'd hurt my mom so much. I was everything to my mom. She made me feel like she'd do anything for me. Anything. It was the best feeling in the world. How could her own mother not feel the exact same way about her?

Paige and I went outside on her small balcony. She tried to make me feel better by joking about her neighbors, but I couldn't pretend that I didn't hear my aunt saying she couldn't handle me alone.

When Aunt Nell showed up in the kitchen, she waved Paige inside. As much as I didn't like living with Ian, it might be better if she went back to him. I didn't think her mom was going to help her and the only other option was for me to go back into foster care. I really didn't want to go back there. I was getting to an age where I'd be sent to the group home instead of another foster family. At the group home, we slept in a large room filled with bunk beds, spent most of the day in a multipurpose room with only one TV that everyone fought over, had to sit through group discussions with guidance counselors, and ate bad fried food. We got to leave for school but that was about it. I tried to stay out of everyone's way, but unless I paid the right girls, I'd be picked on, and not the way Krystal picked on me. Shoved around and beat up. I couldn't go through that again. Aunt Nell had to keep me.

I pulled out my phone and texted Eden. She could make me feel better with one emoticon. I hadn't told her that we'd moved away from Ian yet. I didn't want her possibly telling Caleb if she talked to him. He'd tell his parents who would worry.

She responded almost immediately. She was fighting with her oldest brother over the use of her bathroom. All of her brothers had dates tonight and he'd taken over her bathroom. He was the messiest, so she wasn't too happy. It made me smile. I could almost see her sitting here telling me all about it.

I texted that she should sneak into the bathroom and flush the toilet while he was showering. She responded that her dad was a plumber so obviously he would have fixed that problem. I gave her a few more suggestions just to keep talking to her. She asked how I was doing and when I could come for a visit. I told her everything was okay, and I probably wouldn't be back for a while. I never told her that I probably wouldn't ever be back. At first I didn't know, but now I knew it. Aunt Nell wouldn't be making that drive just so I could visit my friends. She had too much on her plate as it was.

I signed off with Eden. Five seconds later, the phone rang. It was her again.

"I forgot to tell you that my dad said you could come camping with us in a couple of weeks. He said he'd find a place on the coast of Maryland if you can make it so we can swing by and get you on the way. My brothers are less annoying out in the open, and they'll be really nice if you're there."

"I'll ask my aunt, but she's super busy these days." As much as I wanted to go, even though I'd never been camping, I didn't think I could ask Aunt Nell right now.

"Cool. Ask her when you can. I hope you can come with us. My brothers drive me nuts every year. It'd be great to have you there."

"Thanks." I wasn't ready to let her go just yet. "How do the braces feel today? Does your mouth still hurt?"

She groaned. As much as she didn't like the gap in her front teeth, she didn't like the braces even more. "They're total sucko. I can't believe I have to wear them for two years. You're so lucky."

I never thought of straight teeth as lucky, but Eden's simple reasoning made sense. I wanted to see them and convince her they didn't make her look weird, but I'd probably never get the chance. "Sorry they suck. Hope they stop hurting soon."

"Me, too," she agreed. "So is that Ian guy a dorkus?"

I laughed. He was a dorkus. Eden always had the right words for people. "He's okay."

"He doesn't make you decide on his shirt every time he goes out with your aunt does he? I swear my brothers couldn't leave the house without asking me which shirt looks best."

I didn't want to lie to her. "Aunt Nell broke up with him."

"Really?"

"Yeah. They were supposed to get married tomorrow."

"Wow," Eden whistled. "Wasn't it his house?"

"Yeah. We're staying at a friend's while we look for a new place."

She was quiet, more quiet than I'd ever heard her be. "Are you going to be okay there? Can't you just come back and live here?"

"It doesn't work like that. If Aunt Nell couldn't keep me anymore, I'd be placed with a family here in Maryland."

"Oh." She paused again. I wasn't sure she understood what being in foster care was really like. She only knew what it was like for me at M and Briony's. They treated me like I was theirs. "Then I hope you can stay with her. Maybe when things settle down it'll be okay."

"Yeah, it will. I'm not worried." But I was, a lot.

"I'm not either. If you feel like you can't ask her about the camping trip, don't worry. But if she likes to camp, she can come, too."

God, she was nice. I really missed her. "Thanks, Eden."

"Bye, Liv."

I hung up and went inside. Aunt Nell was making dinner. Paige was sitting at the kitchen table looking at her computer. She was looking up apartments again and telling Aunt Nell about the ones that looked good. I guess we were going to be spending Sunday looking for places again.

22

Lauren barely hid her shock when I'd called. Normally Briony made all the phone calls to friends. But Lauren was happy to hear from me. When she heard why I was calling, her customary effervescence erupted. I only hoped that our meeting would be cause for more joy.

"Hi, you two," Jessie greeted us when we arrived at her house.

Briony hugged her hello. I merely nodded. The friends were used to my mile wide personal bubble. She ushered us into her living room where I froze. One, two, three...the counting began automatically. It always did whenever I found myself in an uncomfortable or unexpected situation. This was definitely unexpected. Standing beside the tall, redheaded beauty we expected was her unanticipated best friend, Austy. Exactly my height and size, I shouldn't find her intimidating, but I did. Even more so than her partner, Elise, the FBI agent. Austy always seemed to be touching someone. I feared when she finally felt comfortable around me, she'd extend those touches to me. Twenty-six, twenty-seven...her politeness and consideration made her easy to like. The group certainly adored her as much as they teased her, but each time I tried to get a bead on her, she'd catch me watching her as if she knew exactly what

I was doing and thinking. I found it unnerving, far more than enduring Des's brash comments.

"I hope you don't mind, but I called Aust. She has a good friend who specializes in family law in Maryland. I'm a little out of my depth until I do more research, so I asked for help," Lauren was telling Briony as I snapped out of my paralysis.

I had to be open to anything that would help. If Austy was more familiar with this, I'd gladly push through my anxiety at not knowing her well. Sixty-two, sixty-three…push through, yes, but completely abandon the anxiety, no.

Briony was greeting Austy when Lauren's parents bustled into the living room to say hello. I was pretty sure they were living here now. After Cap broke his hip, Lauren probably didn't want them living on their own anymore. As close as Lauren was to her parents and with Jessie having lost both parents, the cohabitation seemed to work well for them.

"Time for that last checkup, Cap." Jessie popped her head into the living room.

Elise was at her side, twirling a set of car keys on a finger. When she spotted us, she came into the room. "Good to see you, Briony," she reached to shake Briony's hand. We still didn't know them well enough for the hugs that they gave the rest of the group. I was perfectly fine with that.

She turned and set her sights on me. A knot formed in my stomach as I saw that Briony was too far away to do anything. One hundred eighty…I'd have to shake her hand or be unforgivably rude. I could deal with the expected pain, but it might demolish the no-touching constraint I had in place with the group.

Suddenly, Jessie's back appeared in front of me. She diverted Elise's attention by shuttling her and Lauren's parents to the door. I got a passing wave and hello as Elise moved by. Jessie turned back to nod at everyone, her eyes staying on me a second longer before following the group out the door. My breath eased out as I realized she'd done what Briony would have if she could have gotten to me in time. My nerves were frayed about this meeting already. I definitely owed her for keeping them from being obliterated completely.

Briony's eyes met mine with a reassuring smile. Lauren invited us to sit on the couch closest to the beautiful baby grand piano. She and Austy sat on the couch facing us.

"Thanks for taking some of your weekend on this," Briony told the legal duo. "We really appreciate it."

"And want you to bill us," I inserted because I didn't expect them to work for free.

"I wouldn't let either of us do that even if my job allowed it," Austy said with an authority that belied the way the group often teased her.

"Did you have a chance to do some research?" Briony dove right in, probably sensing that I'd already counted well into the three hundreds by now.

"Yes. We both did and Austy made a call to her friend in Maryland."

Briony reached for my hand as we waited for the news. Our last phone call with Olivia had given us hope. Hope that we probably shouldn't have, but it opened the door for the future we'd planned.

Lauren continued, "Unfortunately, it still depends on the aunt. You could petition the court for custody, but you don't have a legal standing with Olivia."

"So basically the same as what we went through here?" Briony asked, defeat thickening her tone. My shoulders fell. I probably shouldn't have suggested we call Lauren when we found out that Olivia's aunt broke off the engagement.

"Yes. I'm sorry. I wish there was something more we could do. I should have recommended you try for legal standing before all of this happened." Lauren looked upset by this omission.

"Please don't take on any guilt for this, Lauren." Briony assured her. "It happened so quickly. We were waiting for school to let out before formalizing things."

"We can't petition for adoption now?" I asked the question outright, even though Lauren had pretty much told us again that we couldn't.

Lauren must have heard the catch in my throat because she looked away and swallowed roughly. Austy spoke up instead. "Not without the blood relative giving up custody."

"What exactly did Olivia tell you?" Lauren asked me about the phone call that prompted this meeting.

"That she and her aunt had moved out and the wedding was off. They were looking for a new apartment, but they weren't having any luck. Knowing her aunt is a payroll clerk, I doubt she can afford much in a suburb of Washington. Her aunt apparently asked her parents for help, but it looks like they refused."

"And you think this means she's considering giving Olivia up?" Lauren asked.

"It's wishful thinking," Briony spoke our hopes out loud. "It's likely that she only took Olivia in because she was getting married. She thought her life would be stable, and now it's turned upside down. She's barely out of college. Most people that age living near a city need a roommate to make ends meet. Taking care of a kid may be too much for her."

Lauren nodded. "I hope you're right."

"She's trying to be brave, but she's reverting," I added because it seemed vital that they know why we thought we might have a chance here. "She doesn't talk much on the phone, and she's been on the verge of crying more than once."

"She's losing herself there," Briony summed up our viewpoint. "It might just be an adjustment period, but I don't want her to lose hold of that amazing girl she was with us."

Austy leaned forward and asked gently, "Have you spoken to the aunt?" Her posture gave the impression that she was eager for the answer no matter who responded or what might be said. It must win her a lot of favor in court. According to the group's gossip, Austy had more wins in court than Lauren.

"No. We tried when she was here, but she wasn't interested in meeting us."

"You could try calling her," Austy suggested.

"We could call her on your behalf," Lauren suggested instead.

Austy shook her head and placed her hand on Lauren's arm. "It would be better if it came from them. That way it doesn't seem adversarial."

"That's why she was valedictorian," Lauren tilted her head in Austy's direction and beamed at us.

"I was not," Austy shot back, red flushing her cheeks.

"She's right," Lauren talked over her friend's embarrassment. "The next time you're on the phone with Olivia, ask to say hello to the aunt. Have a few phone calls like that just to get acquainted. You might find out a little more about her frame of mind."

Briony and I nodded at her suggestion. That would probably be the best way to approach this. It would take time and might not produce any results, but Austy was right. If we accused her of not being able to take care of Olivia anymore, she could cut off all contact.

"Do we have a chance of getting her back now that she's in Maryland?" I was worried about that detail, too.

"If she re-entered the foster system, you would have to be a registered foster family in Maryland," Austy told us. "My friend tells me it's a much shorter process since you already qualify here."

"If it comes to adoption," Lauren took up the conversation. "Her being in Maryland actually helps you since they're more open to all family types there. You'll have two options. There's public adoption out of the foster care system, or private adoption that would deal directly with the aunt. Public adoption can take a year or two, and it'll be more difficult with you living out of state. Private adoption doesn't take as long, but it's costly because you're paying for the home study and other fees."

We nodded again, looking at each other. We expected the private route would be the best option and knew it would be costly. Briony and I made good money, but I didn't know what a lawyer thought was expensive. If we had to, we could take out a second mortgage or maybe I'd swallow my pride and finally ask Willa for a loan.

"Try to talk to the aunt then private adoption if that's what comes of it?" Briony summed everything up.

"It's your best path," Austy told us. Her eyes landed on mine. "You must miss her terribly. I wish we could offer a different solution, but family law is complicated."

Complicated and not always justified. If we'd been Olivia's aunts, no judge would have ruled in favor of a twenty-four-year-old woman with one year of work experience now sharing an apartment with a friend.

Once again, I couldn't help but think this was my fault. If Briony and I had started the adoption process when we first discussed it, we might have been able to fight in court. We might not have retained custody because the courts place way too much emphasis on blood relations, but we could have fought the immediate placement.

I stood, not wanting to take up more of their weekend. "We appreciate what you've found out. Thank you both."

"You're welcome. Please let us know what comes of this. I can draw up the papers and represent you if it goes your way," Lauren offered.

"Thanks, Laur. You're the best." Briony leaned in for a hug. "Austy, we appreciate you working on this."

Their news wasn't as good as we'd hoped, but now we had an action plan to follow. It might not go anywhere, but we had to give it a try.

23

Olivia   It was hard to sleep. Paige didn't keep the air-conditioner on at night so I kept waking up and kicking off my covers. Plus they were still up talking. They did this after they thought I was asleep. We hadn't found a place yet. Now we were looking for a two bedroom with a den that she and Paige could share. Paige couldn't move out for another month, but they'd be able to afford a better place if they were both going to live there. They said they could fit a bed into a den space for me, so we'd all have our own rooms. I guess it was better than a one bedroom for my aunt and the couch for me.

I rolled to the edge of the pullout couch and reached down for my backpack. My fingers skimmed the sturdy material. I'd been doing this a lot lately. The texture seemed to help whenever I felt all tangled up inside. Touching something that was mine, something that came with a lot of good memories. It was almost like I could relive the happy day I got it again.

It felt like it was a hundred degrees in here. It didn't help having to listen to them rehashing all the stuff they didn't like about the last apartment we looked at. Unzipping one of the interior compartments, I pulled out my memory book. Almost every page had a picture of my mom, some with me, one with her and Aunt Nell, one with all of us. I flipped past the remaining blank pages to the last few. When I'd been stuck in my bedroom at Ian's, I decided to add photos of my time with Briony and M. They'd made copies of all the photos they took of us and gave them to me. I kept some on my phone and added the best to the book. I'd look at these for a few minutes and try to get back to sleep.

Or I thought I would, until I heard them change the topic from crappy apartments to something else.

"What do you think they want?" Paige asked.

My aunt's voice didn't carry as well as Paige's, but I could still hear their conversation from the end of the hall. "I don't know. They say just a visit, but what if it's something more?"

Who would be visiting? Their friends? Aunt Nell's parents? What was the something more they could want? Were they going to try to convince Aunt Nell to give me up like they did with my mom? Sleeping on a pullout couch in hundred degree temps and overhearing every word people said in the apartment wasn't as bad as being sent back to the unknown of foster care. I'd sleep on a couch for the rest of my life if it meant I wouldn't have to spend any more time in a group home.

"What if they do? Would that be so bad?"

"Wouldn't it? What if they're like Ian says?"

Paige laughed in a sarcastic way. "Ian's a hypocrite. You can't believe anything he said. It's not like I know a whole lot of them, but the ones I've met seem okay. Definitely nothing like Ian's been preaching."

"You really think they'd be good for her?"

I was trying to follow what they were saying. It sounded like they were talking about me, but they kept saying 'they' and not using my name. It could be about their college friends. They talked about them a lot. Ian hadn't liked many of Aunt Nell's college friends.

"If they'd been bad for her, I don't think she'd be this good."

"What about the guilt?"

"I was there, Nell, remember? You were devastated when Nina died. You couldn't do anything then, and you've felt guilty ever since. It's why you let Ian rush you into it. He had an idea of a perfect family and a warped view once he found out about them. She likes them. Everything she said about them tells me they're good people. Hell, it sounded better than my childhood."

They were definitely talking about me, but I still couldn't understand what they meant. Why was Paige bringing this up now? Did something happen today that made Aunt Nell feel extra guilty about not wanting me at first? Was a social worker coming by again? Someone visited a week after we'd moved into Ian's, but Aunt Nell said that would be the last time since she was my guardian not a foster parent. Maybe she'd been wrong.

"I don't know," Aunt Nell groaned.

"Let's just see, okay?" Paige encouraged her. "It can't hurt. If you don't feel good about them, then that's it. But it may work out for you."

Somehow that didn't feel all that encouraging to me.

24

Olivia Paige's boyfriend was tapping his keys against his leg, impatient. Aunt Nell and Paige were still in the bathroom getting ready for us to go out to lunch. They were taking forever. I didn't blame Dillon for being impatient.

"You excited?" he asked me.

Excited? For what? Lunch? Paige and Aunt Nell stopped for lunch while looking at apartments all the time. Maybe we were going someplace special. Maybe that was why they were taking so long to get ready.

Before I could ask what he meant, they finally came out of the bathroom and started herding us to the door. All of a sudden we were in a rush. I'd learned to just go with the flow whenever adults started acting weird.

We headed to a restaurant that'd we'd gone to before. It wasn't any place fancy. Not worth all that time they spent getting ready in the bathroom. I wish my jeans didn't have a hole in them, but Paige didn't have a sewing kit to patch them up. I was going to have to buy one the next time we went to the store.

Inside, Dillon went up to the hostess stand and we waited while she gathered some menus. Aunt Nell put her arm around my shoulders and guided me in front of her. That was a little weird. Usually she and Paige would go where they needed to go and I'd be following behind.

"Livy!"

I stopped in my tracks. That sounded like Caleb, but he wouldn't be here. My eyes raced around the restaurant anyway. I spotted him in two seconds. He was standing beside a table near the back window. Briony and M were there, too. I couldn't believe it. My heart started pounding and I felt like I might cry. I didn't think I'd ever see them again.

Caleb started toward me, but Briony stood and held onto his arm, leaning over to whisper at him. He stepped back and waved wildly at me. I waved back. My smile stretched so wide it hurt my face. I was so glad to see them.

"Surprise," Aunt Nell said from behind me. "Is this okay?"

Is this okay? It's the best thing ever. Why didn't she tell me? "It's great," I practically shouted with glee. I didn't care if this would only last an hour. I never thought I'd be with them again. I'd take everything I could from this visit.

Aunt Nell drew in a breath and nodded. She seemed to need a second before she started toward their table. She'd only just started talking to them on the phone a couple of weeks ago. At first it was just hello, but the last two times I spoke to Briony, she'd talked to Aunt Nell for a few minutes each time. They must have been planning this lunch surprise.

When I reached the table I didn't even have time to say hi before Briony wrapped me in her arms. "It's so good to see you, sweetie."

I squeezed her hard, pouring every minute I'd missed her into the hug. She felt exactly the same, like safety and warmth and home all in one, and she smelled the same, like trees in the woods where we'd take hikes sometimes. Soft and strong and a world champion hugger.

Too soon she let go, but it was to hold her hand out to my aunt. "Hello, Nell, it's nice to meet you in person."

Caleb reached over and gave me a hug that was a series of gentle back slaps. He talked a mile a minute, so fast that I could barely understand him. I was still dazed from the surprise and missed most of what he was saying.

Over his shoulder, I saw M step forward and shake Aunt Nell's hand. My eyes widened at the sight. She didn't shake peoples' hands, not unless she had to. My principal, my social worker, my teacher, but she'd let Briony do all the other greeting for them.

"Nice to meet you both," Briony was telling Paige and Dillon as M came over to me.

When she leaned down and hugged me, tears pushed at my eyes. I didn't want them to see how sad I'd been and how much I'd missed them, so I blinked them away. It wouldn't be a nice thing to do to Aunt Nell, either. I just concentrated on how good it felt to be in M's arms again. Briony was all safety and warmth in her hugs. M gave reassurance that everything would be okay in hers. She smelled like clean linen fresh from the dryer. A little leaner than Briony, she always felt more strong than soft, but I loved her hugs just as much.

"Hi, Olivia. We've missed you so much."

I nodded my head against her shoulder and finally released her. I didn't want to get too used to these hugs again. It had taken me weeks before I stopped remembering how they felt every night.

Briony ran her fingers over my hair while I was in M's embrace. She turned to gesture for everyone to take a seat around the table. "We're so glad you all could make it today. We've been looking forward to this for weeks."

I jerked back in surprise. They'd been planning this get together for weeks? Briony must have caught my shock because her smile faltered.

"Your aunt must be really good at keeping surprises, huh?" she said to me before telling everyone, "I was always lousy at it. Caleb says he can find any present I try to hide the second I hide it."

I felt numb as Caleb pulled me into a seat next to him. He bumped my shoulder and said hello again. He looked happy, like he pretty much always looked. He looked tan, too. He'd spent a lot of time outside this summer. I bet Hank and Eden looked the same way. It suddenly became real how different my summer was from the one we'd planned.

After we ordered, Briony and M made small talk with my aunt and her friends. I kept watching Aunt Nell, feeling her nerves from beside me. She was halfway through her meal before she finally started to relax. Briony was good at getting people to talk.

"Hey, I just realized who you are." Dillon was looking directly at M. She stiffened in her chair but kept an open smile on her face. "You taught that ops management class I took at UVA one summer. That was a killer class. Paige, you remember me talking about that. I loved that class. You were great."

"Oh, thanks. I'm glad you liked it," M responded quietly. This wasn't the first time we'd run into former students. She always seemed amazed that they'd remember her.

Aunt Nell shot him a look like he'd just jumped on M's side. Why was she upset with him? Were there sides here?

"Are you visiting the area or just passing through?" Paige asked when Aunt Nell's glare cut Dillon off.

"We're headed up to Vermont to visit my parents," Briony told her. "Flying out of Dulles."

"We're a bit out of the way here," Paige pointed out.

Briony smiled at her then looked at me. "It's not too far for a visit with this one. We're so happy to see you, Livy."

I nodded and smiled. My throat was tight. With the move to my aunt's and the breakup with Ian, I'd forgotten about the trip to see Caleb's grandparents and aunts. Their plan was to get permission from my social worker so I could go with them. They couldn't get it for Christmas because my social worker had been sick and her replacement rejected the request. I thought they'd go anyway because they always went home at Christmas, but they didn't. And since Briony and Caleb weren't coming to them, her whole family came to us. That was a way cool thing to do, and everyone was super nice to me. I'd hoped to get to see them again this summer.

"When does school start here?" Caleb asked me.

I frowned and looked at my aunt. I didn't know. I didn't even know what school I was going to be in. It was still a month away, but I wanted to know now.

"We're still deciding on a place to live," Aunt Nell said. "We'll know as soon as we find a place."

Briony glanced at M with worry in her eyes. "Probably after labor day like yours, Caleb."

"Finding apartments is never fun, especially in a city," M offered.

"We're looking for a big enough place for all of us," Aunt Nell said. "We're trying to find the best place, right, Livy?"

I nodded and tried to smile, but I was afraid I might tear up if I did. None of the places we looked at last weekend were good. Not one even had a den or a living room big enough for a pullout couch for me to sleep on. I tried not to think about my beautiful room at Briony and M's. I tried to not think about how I didn't have to ask permission to get a snack or check to make sure which food in the fridge was ours and which was Paige's. I tried not to think about how I'd nearly wet my pants several mornings because one of them was hogging the one and only bathroom. It wouldn't do me any good to remember that Briony and M treated me just like my mom had, not as an afterthought.

Briony asked Aunt Nell about her work again. That seemed to fill in the rest of the lunch. I felt like my time with them was slipping away, but there wasn't anything I could do to stop it.

We all walked outside together. Briony thanked them again for agreeing to the lunch. "We're going to the Smithsonian tomorrow. We'd love to have you all join us."

My hopes soared. I didn't care if we'd watch grass grow together as long as I got to see them again.

"I don't think so, but thank you," Aunt Nell crushed my hopes in a sentence.

"Would you like to join us for dinner and a movie tomorrow night? We're on a plane first thing Monday morning. It would be so great to spend more time with Liv."

Aunt Nell looked at Paige for a moment. I couldn't tell what they were thinking and crossed my fingers that she'd agree. I loved museums and having Caleb there with me would be awesome. Briony and M would make it fun and interesting, but my aunt wouldn't be into that. She never talked about going to museums for fun. She and Paige liked shopping and dancing for fun.

Aunt Nell tilted her chin up and said, "Maybe when you come back from Vermont."

My eyes widened. They were coming back? Here?

Briony's face split into a wide smile. "That sounds great, Nell. Thank you. We've missed your niece so much."

Aunt Nell's arm wrapped around me again. "She's pretty great."

My heart pumped harder. That was the first time Aunt Nell spoke like she was happy to have me around. Since ditching Ian, she hadn't been full of compliments for anyone.

"She's the best," Caleb agreed and my aunt smiled. I think she was starting to like him.

"We won't keep you. If you change your mind about dinner or the movie tomorrow, you have our number." Briony turned to me and swooped in for another hug. "Good to see you, sweetie. You've been having fun with your aunt, I can tell."

I had to hide my surprise. I thought she could tell that I hadn't been having fun living here. Both she and M were always good at telling when Caleb and I weren't really into something. I guess I should be glad she didn't know that I desperately wished I never had to leave their home. That for the first time since my mom died, I didn't think of it as their home. I thought of it as my home.

Caleb hugged me next. "It's going to be so boring with just the 'rents tomorrow." I laughed because I knew he was just acting tough. He loved hanging out with his mom and stepmom.

M hugged me. "It was wonderful to see you. Text or call whenever you can. We miss talking to you. Nell, it was great to meet you. You too, Paige, and Dillon, nice to see you again."

"Same here, Professor D." He called her by what she was known at school. Paige elbowed him but kept smiling at them.

"If we don't hear from you tomorrow, we'll call before our flight back," Briony told Nell.

She shook her hand and we watched them head to M's car. They turned and waved as they piled in. It was crazy, but I missed them already.

"I can't believe you were living with Professor D. She was the best prof I've ever had."

"She was that good?" Aunt Nell asked him.

"She's like a mentor, a story teller, and teacher all wrapped up into one. Bet she was fun at home?" he asked me.

"She was," I said before I lost my nerve and thought that Aunt Nell might get upset to hear that I had a good time living there.

"You liked living with them? You didn't mind living with strangers?" Paige asked.

What was I supposed to say? Paige was a stranger, but I was living with her. "They made me feel welcome right away. No other house did that. They asked me if I wanted to stay with them, too. None of the other families asked."

"And you didn't mind that they're, you know, gay?" Aunt Nell asked.

I frowned, thinking that was a stupid question. Them being gay had nothing to do with me. "They acted like any of the other couples I stayed with, except they actually love each other and get along. All the other families fought a lot and didn't really seem like they loved each other anymore."

"But do they try to, you know, get you to like girls? You don't, do you?" Aunt Nell said, shooting a glance at her friend.

"They wouldn't do that. That's—" I cut myself off before I insulted her by saying it was a stupid thing to say. Stupid that she thought someone could make that happen and stupid that she thought Briony or M would force me to like girls. "I'm not into stuff like that anyway."

"But you will be. Boy crazy, I mean, you should be. I was at your age, so was your mom."

I frowned. Either she didn't know my mom very well or she was lying. My mom told me that she hadn't kissed a boy until she was fifteen. She wasn't even interested until the guy who was my father wanted to date her. She said that her mom never told her anything about sex, so when it happened, she wasn't prepared. That was the reason she'd explained sex to me not long before she died. She wanted me to be aware and prepared. But she always made a big deal out of telling me that she wanted me even if I hadn't been planned. Even if having me meant her family turned their backs on her. I never doubted that.

Aunt Nell pressed her lips together, shooting another glance at Paige.

"They do seem really together, Nell."

"I know Professor D is," Dillon put in.

"Maybe," was all Aunt Nell would agree to.

25

Briony's mother, Susan, was currently arguing with two of the grandkids over naptime. The two littlest in the litter still had to endure the torture of a nap while all the other grandkids got to continue playing together. What amazed me the most was that these two weren't actually her grandkids. They were Allison's, Caleb's other grandmother, but that didn't matter around here. Briony called it the Vermont compound. Both sets of grandparents lived a few blocks away from each other, and Caleb's two aunts were within five minutes of Susan's. Whenever Caleb came back to town, all the grandchildren got together at every location, no matter the relation.

Tomorrow the kids would be going to Allison's house. Three of the kids were still in day camp every day, but the rest of the kids would spend the last few weeks of summer bouncing from one house to the next in the compound. In the eight days we'd been here, Briony and I hosted the kids at the hotel pool almost every day. It wasn't quite the relaxing getaway we'd hoped for, but so far I didn't mind.

We were leaving tomorrow. Nine days was enough for Briony and more than enough for me. Caleb would stay with his grandparents until school started, but Briony and I usually took the rest of the summer for a short vacation and some alone time at home. This year, we were going to Boston so Briony could show me around her old haunts.

Arms slid around my middle from behind me. Instantly I recognized the scent and feel of Briony. Three years ago I would have incapacitated anyone who got this close to me, much less touched me. Today, touch was still hard for me, still painful from anyone other than my family. I could steel myself for these trips when Briony's whole family, especially the kids, would all hug, touch, poke, prod, push, pull, and grab me. Knowing they meant each touch with care, it was easier to tolerate. It seemed to get easier and easier each year. I wondered if the pain would fade completely after enough of these visits. It had with Briony and Caleb and Olivia.

"Hi, sexy," Briony whispered and kissed the spot just below my ear. "Ready to skip town yet?"

I chuckled. I knew she didn't mean right now, but for a fleeting moment, the idea appealed. Poor Susan. She was losing the naptime battle. "I know we planned to leave, but if you wanted to stay, it's not like we don't have a flexible schedule."

Briony sighed, probably both happy that I was willing to stay near her family and depressed that part of the reason we had a flexible schedule was because Olivia was with her aunt now. "We can always come back and pick Caleb up, but I'm okay with leaving tomorrow."

I nodded, leaning back into her embrace. We'd help Susan in a moment, but for now I'd just stand here until the moment was up. Playing the director of fun over the last week helped ease the pain of the reopened wound at seeing Olivia and not getting the most encouraging vibe from her aunt on the visit.

As petty as it seemed, I'd hoped that we'd find Nell more distracted and less wary. I didn't think she'd figured out that we were angling for more than just a day or two of visits with her niece. Briony thought she might have caught on. There were certainly enough secret looks between Nell and Paige.

We'd confirmed our suspicions that Olivia was back to being the inhibited girl she was when she first moved in with us. She hadn't said more than a few sentences at lunch. And she nearly cried when Briony tried to cheer her up with some encouraging words about how much fun she was having with her aunt. As if we couldn't tell she wasn't happy. The flash of disappointment on her face when she thought we didn't know how she felt anymore was heartbreaking.

We weren't giving up all hope. Nell agreed to meet with us on our way back from the airport. That was hopeful. At the very least, we wanted to float the idea of spending more time in Olivia's life. But the ultimate goal was to follow Austy's advice and broach the subject of adoption. Nell hadn't acted like a selfish twenty-something who only thought of herself, but she wasn't the mother that Briony was. Not even the mother that I was.

"What are you thinking about?"

I shrugged and smiled, caught. Briony knew what I was thinking about, surrounded by kids having fun, included in a loving family. "Do you ever miss living here?" I hadn't been thinking of that, but the thought just entered my head. She must. Her folks showed concern and care and love with every action, her former sisters-in-law treated her like a real sister that they desperately missed and loved, and her former in-laws could easily be mistaken for her parents.

She gripped my chin and turned my head to look at her. "I do, but I wouldn't give away my time in Virginia for anything. I relish teaching there, I adore our friends, and I found you when I never thought I'd love again. I found someone who fits me perfectly and loves my son and makes my life happy and whole."

I turned to face her, smiling at the truth of her statement.

"I didn't have all that before, you know." Her eyes darted over to gage the hearing distance to her nieces and nephews. "That happens when you marry young. I don't know how I'd be now if I was still here, but I know I've never been happier than I am with you."

My eyes misted. "I feel the same way about you. I know how I'd be without you, and I wouldn't like it at all."

She leaned in and brushed her lips over mine. "Let's go deal with naptime for Mom then we'll get the rest of the troupes set for an afternoon at the park. Give Mom and Dad their last break of the summer before we dart out of here tomorrow."

Boston tomorrow, reliving some of Briony's past. Getting to know her even better. It probably wouldn't be possible to love her more, but I never say never with Briony in my life.

26

MWe were meeting in the hotel restaurant. We'd suggested the room we were staying in for more privacy, but Nell wouldn't go for it. I wondered if our being lesbians had something to do with her comfort level. If so, we'd be in for an unproductive meeting today. As it was, I'd barely slept all night, too hyped about what we were trying to accomplish today.

"Hi, Nell, thanks for taking the time to come by," Briony greeted her when she came into our booth. We were in the far corner, meeting at a time when the restaurant was slow. "It's nice to see you again."

"You, too," Nell said and shook Briony's hand before turning to me.

Her palm slid against mine. The discomfort started out as a shock from static electricity. It always did. If it were just that, I wouldn't need to avoid handshakes. But soon it would flare to something more painful like multiple cat scratches. I could almost always end the contact before it progressed to the agony of swarming bee stings. Thankfully, Nell didn't seem to want to prolong the handshake any more than I did.

"How are you doing?" Briony jumped in to pull Nell's focus away in case I flinched at her touch. "Work going okay?"

Nell looked at her for a minute then said, "What exactly are you looking for here?"

I tried to remember that she must love Olivia as much as we did even though she barely knew her and that she was probably feeling a little defensive. But it didn't help much when she talked to my partner like that.

"Okay, we'll get right to it." Briony turned to me for an encouraging look. "We miss Olivia. She became part of our family when she was with us. We'd hoped to make that permanent."

Nell looked like she was going to say something but thought better of it.

"We were very sad but also very glad when you came for her. We obviously didn't want to lose her, but it would be good for her to know her mom's sister again. She misses her mom so much. You must miss her, too."

Nell's eyes shimmered, but she didn't say anything.

"When Olivia told us your engagement was off, we knew things would get harder for you."

She sat up straighter. "I can do fine for myself."

"Of course you can. I meant that I know how hard it is to be a single parent. I was for four years, and it was the hardest time of my life. I had a lot of help from my family, but still, it wasn't what I'd planned when my late partner and I had our son." Briony gave her a reassuring smile. "I thought that maybe your plans might have gotten a little turned around when you broke up with your fiancé."

Nell nodded, letting out a breath. "I'm not going to lie. The only reason I thought I could raise Olivia was because I was getting married and we wanted to start a family. I can do it alone, but no, you're right, it wasn't what I'd envisioned when I petitioned for her."

"We understand." Briony gave me a brief hopeful look then turned back to Nell. "Let me just tell you what we hoped for and then we'll leave you to think things over. Before you petitioned for her, we wanted to adopt Olivia. We still want to."

"That's not...I don't..." Nell couldn't form her thoughts.

"We don't want to take her away from you," I inserted and Nell shot her surprised gaze to me.

"How is adopting her not taking her away from me?"

"You're her aunt. You'll always be her aunt. We'd want you to be part of her life, as much as you'd want to be." I clarified and looked at Briony to make sure I sounded nonthreatening.

Nell's eyes shifted back and forth between us. The wariness hadn't left her expression yet. "How do you see that working?"

Briony glanced at me before answering, "Any way you want it to, Nell."

Nell's brow furrowed. "I never...maybe it could...I don't know."

"Did you see Olivia a lot with her mom?" I stepped in, hoping I could steer her toward what she should already know. She was Olivia's aunt, not her parent. She might have tried when she was getting married, but alone, barely out of college, needing a roommate to afford a two bedroom apartment, it would be much more difficult than she imagined.

She considered how to answer my question. Olivia gave the impression that it wasn't a regular occurrence seeing her aunt. "Not often. When I went to college, we lived in the same town. So a little more then."

"Did you ever babysit for Olivia?" I asked.

"No." She shook her head, brow furrowing. "Nina always had child care covered."

"Then it would be safe to say that your sister wouldn't have expected you to be anything other than her aunt if she hadn't passed away?"

"There'd be no need," Nell agreed.

"And if Olivia had a safe, permanent home where she was loved and well cared for, would your sister want you to be anything more than Olivia's aunt?"

She swallowed, blinking back tears. As we'd suspected, guilt that she'd survived her sister and loyalty had made her step up to take care of Olivia. The harsh reality of parenting took a back seat when she'd had help and support from her fiancé. She glanced at me then at Briony, who probably looked more sympathetic even though I was trying my best. "I can't be sure."

"No," Briony took the hint and continued my line of reasoning. "But you can be assured that Olivia will be well taken care of and cherished in our home. You'll be able to call her and have access to her just as if you were calling your sister's home."

Silence hit us from the other side of the booth. I should have sat us at a four top so Briony and I wouldn't look like we were on one side and she was on the other.

Nell took a full minute before she spoke. "I don't think it's right for me to just drop her on you. I know she likes you. That's clear, but it doesn't mean I should just drop all responsibility."

"You won't be," Briony denied. "Aunts have responsibility. Now that you've come back into her life, she'll need you, always."

"You make it sound so easy." Her eyes drifted off toward the windows lining the front of the restaurant. "It shouldn't be easy to walk away from this."

"It won't be easy, and you won't be walking away. There may be times when we can't drive up to meet you or match up school vacations. We're going to have to work together to make it so we're all a part of her life. I don't get to see my nieces and nephews very often, but I do feel like I'm a big part of their life. We'd want the same with you. As much as you'd want."

"How can I..." she started but couldn't seem to finish.

"Tell her?" I guessed. Hope surged for the first time all day.

"If we were to do this, yes. She's been moved all over from what I can tell. Yours was the only place she stayed at for more than four months. She's only been with me for two."

"We'd like to be there to talk to her with you," Briony said. "To be honest, we haven't talked to her about adoption. We'd planned to do that this summer, but you came back into her life, so we never got around to broaching the subject."

Nell's mouth popped open. "Are you saying you don't even know if she'd be okay with it?"

"Not exactly. We're sure that she liked living with us. She asked if she could stay when your petition came through."

Nell glared at Briony.

Briony waved her hands to assure her she hadn't meant any insult. "Only because she didn't really know what it would be like with you. Kids don't like change any more than we do. She made some good friends in Charlottesville, and she gets along really well with Caleb. We think she'd like to come back."

"I don't know. We're doing okay. Once we find the right apartment, we'll be great."

That wasn't what we wanted to hear. I thought we'd begun to swing her around to the idea of being the aunt she was supposed to be and letting us be parents, but it sounded like she was building a wall again. In fact, I didn't think we could even ask to see Olivia tomorrow like we'd planned based on the tone she was using now. We'd have to hope she held true to her word that we could see Olivia when Caleb came back from Vermont at the end of the summer.

"It's a lot to think about, we know," Briony told her. She was good at making people feel okay with being unsure. "We don't expect you to decide anything now. We just wanted you to know how much we love your niece and want her in our lives."

She could have said so much more. How much Olivia loved living with us. How she begged us not to make her leave. How her grades flourished and worry vanished in our home. Every bit of proof we had that Olivia was better off with us than an aunt who was having a hard time taking care of herself right now. But that was the difference between Briony and me. I might have said some of those things and probably gotten Nell's defenses up and shut down all future possibilities to even talk to Olivia much less see her.

"Okay," Nell said and nodded at us. "I'm glad...that is, she thinks a lot of you. Thank you for stepping in when her family wasn't able to."

Wasn't able to? They refused. Sure, Nell was just a junior in college. It would have been tough, but many, many others had done it before.

"She's been a blessing to us," Briony said as her eyes dimmed at the finality in Nell's tone. We'd made our plea for Olivia's sake, for our sake, for a future that included Olivia, and Nell thanked us for what we'd done in the past.

It wasn't a certainty, but the way Nell was acting, our adoption hope was going to stay a hope indefinitely.

27

Olivia Trying not to cry feels almost as bad as crying. I'd been fighting the urge since I woke up extra early. I wanted to be awake when my aunt was getting ready for work. It was too much to hope that she'd take the day off, but I really thought she'd at least say something while we were having breakfast. When she didn't, when all she did was rush through a bowl of cereal and a cup of coffee, when she didn't even ask why I was up before she left for work, I swallowed everything I planned to tell her.

I was supposed to get my ears pierced today. I was supposed to have cake and ice cream and go to the movies or the zoo or a museum or whatever I wanted to do because that's what my mom had planned for my twelfth birthday.

She would wake me up like she did every year with a cheery, "Wakey, wakey, birthday girl. It's your special day." It didn't matter if it was a work day. She'd always take the day off to spend with me. Most birthdays it was just us having fun. She'd try to make each one special, but it was my twelfth birthday that she'd planned for me to get my ears pierced.

As if my birthday could be worse without my mom here, Aunt Nell hadn't said anything. She was always quiet in the morning, so I thought she just needed a little time to get her coffee working. But she placed her mug in the sink and gathered her bag and slipped on her heels and told me to have a nice day like usual. Then she walked out the door without saying anything. She forgot that today was my birthday.

 For the first time since my mom died I'd been looking forward to a birthday because finally I was with someone who cared. Briony had been planning my day since Caleb's birthday in March. When I told her about Mom's plan, she was as excited as I was about getting my ears pierced. I thought I'd get as close to a Mom birthday as I could get without her here. Then Aunt Nell came along and it's been tough, but I thought she'd remember. She used to send cards and she'd spent two birthdays with me before Mom died. But this morning, nothing. It was just another day for her, and I couldn't just tell her because it wouldn't mean anything. It would be just like at those other foster homes when they found out my birthday had passed while I lived with them. A promise to do something next year when we all knew that I'd never be with them next year.

 Paige surfaced from her bedroom looking professional. "Hey, Livy, I'm off to a client meeting. You're on your own for the day. Don't party too hard," she joked as she dashed out the door.

 I waited until I heard her car start up before I let my tears fall. This wasn't fair. Aunt Nell took me from the best home I could ever have and I didn't complain. She made me live with her dorky boyfriend, who turned out to be a jerk, and I didn't complain. She moved us into an apartment that was hardly big enough for one person, and I'm really trying not to complain. But forgetting a day I'd been looking forward to for four years since Mom first mentioned what she had planned, it was too much.

I tried not to be selfish, Aunt Nell was going through a lot, but shouldn't she remember her niece's birthday?

My phone buzzed. The apartment was so quiet that I could hear my phone buzzing from the living room even when I was blowing my nose in the bathroom. I didn't feel like talking to anyone, but it might be Aunt Nell.

"Happy Birthday, Olivia!" Briony and M sang through the line.

Tears came to my eyes again as I listened to them sing the entire song. I wiped them away and swiped another tissue under my nose.

"What are you guys up to today, sweetie?" Briony asked.

"Um," I hesitated because like my mom, Briony and M planned to take the day off and celebrate with me. We were going to bake a cake in the morning, then Briony and M were taking me to the mall to get my ears pierced, and after that we were going to the zoo with Caleb, Hank, and Eden. The zoo was one of my favorite places. Caleb would have told me to ask for an amusement park, but he liked the zoo almost as much. Then we'd go out to dinner and come home for cake and ice cream and Eden was going to spend the night. It was more than my mom had ever planned for me. I'd been looking forward to it since the day after Caleb's birthday when we started planning mine. Instead I was listening to them sing to me on the phone and ask what my aunt was going to do for me. I hoped they didn't think less of Aunt Nell because she hadn't taken the day off. "Aunt Nell had to work, and Paige just left for a meeting."

There was a brief pause before Briony's bright voice came back with, "I'll bet they have something big planned after work. Maybe dinner out or something really fun?"

No chance of that, but I couldn't really say that to the two women who would have made this day really special for me. "Probably," I replied with as much fake enthusiasm as I could muster. They didn't need to know that my aunt had forgotten my birthday.

"Did you get our gift yet?" M asked. "We set the delivery date for today."

"Oh, you guys didn't have to get me anything." But darn it, I was really glad they had.

"Of course we did, honey. You don't turn twelve every day," Briony said. "We wish we could be there to see you open it."

"Me, too. Thank you so much." We talked a little more about what I'd been doing and how their trip was and every word made me sadder. I hoped that they were going to stop by for a visit when they got back, but they didn't mention it. As much as I loved talking to them, maybe I shouldn't do this anymore. Maybe I should send Willa's phone back so I wouldn't be tempted to talk to them again.

About an hour after that call, Willa called and Quinn texted, then I got a text from Jessie and Lauren, several texts and calls from Eden, a text and a call from Caleb, and a text from Hank. I missed them all so much.

After lunch, UPS knocked on the door and handed me a package. I smiled wide, not just because I knew this was Briony and M's gift, but because this was my first package ever. Aunt Nell used to send me cards when I lived with Mom, but I'd never gotten a package before.

I took my time opening the box. Stuffed inside lots of colorful tissue paper was a small gift wrapped box. Unwrapping the present, I felt a little excitement return. The black velvet box brought on the tears again. I knew what it was before I opened it. Two peridot stones blinked at me, nestled into the velvet. The gold posts would have been perfect for newly healed pierced ears. Peridot, my birthstone, I felt a mixture of sadness and joy. I'd be selfish for as long as Briony and M wanted to keep contacting me. It would be a reward for the lousy foster homes and the absentminded aunt I'd lived with so far.

By the time Aunt Nell got home after work, I'd gotten over feeling bad that she didn't remember my birthday. None of my foster homes had celebrated, I never thought I'd get another birthday party. Just because Briony and M had planned a big day for me didn't mean I should have planned for something like that to actually happen.

Some kids get birthday parties, and some kids get to live with their aunt who is doing everything she can to keep them safe. Birthday parties weren't everything. No one would be like my mom and no one would be like Briony and M. I just needed to get that, so my expectations were at the right level from now on.

28

Olivia The neighbor was washing his sports car again. He washed it every week and barely drove it. His six and eight-year-old kids didn't even fit in it, so I wasn't sure why he owned it. Paige called it his mid-life crisis car.

I glanced up toward his unit, wondering where his kids were. Usually they'd be up trying to douse each other with the hose. It was pretty funny to watch, which was why I was sitting on the staircase waiting. They should be up, but no sounds were coming from his open windows. He probably switched weekends with his ex-wife or something.

He was buffing the wax from the bright red paint job, almost done. It would be another two hours before any of the other kids in the complex were up and about. Two boys a little older than me always kicked a soccer ball around the parking lot for an hour or so. It reminded me of kicking the ball around with Caleb in the backyard. He always had suggestions for something to do. We played catch as much as we kicked the soccer ball or used the net in the backyard to play volleyball and badminton. If the boys were half as nice as Caleb, I'd ask to play with them, but they were kind of intimidating. At least they didn't make any comments when they caught me watching them.

This past week had been really boring. Caleb was busy with his cousins in Vermont. Hank was at a sleep away camp, and Eden was in Germany visiting her mom. No one had any spare time to text, and it wouldn't change for another week.

I stood from the steps and headed back to the apartment. Aunt Nell slept in on Saturdays, but we only had the next two weekends to find an apartment otherwise I'd have to start school around here and possibly move to another school when they found the right place. If I made coffee, that usually woke her up.

Paige was already in the kitchen when I came inside. It looked like she was on her second cup of coffee. She and Aunt Nell had gone to Dillon's for a couple of hours last night, and Aunt Nell came back without her. She tipped her head at me and immediately pressed a palm to her forehead. I knew that gesture. She had a hangover. That meant Aunt Nell might have one, too. We'd be lucky to see any apartments today.

I heard Aunt Nell's door open and tilted back to watch her duck into the bathroom. Paige poured a cup of coffee and walked it down the hall. She tapped on the door twice, opened it, and set the mug on the vanity before coming back toward me.

"Coffee?" she asked me.

I frowned. I never knew if she was joking or if she thought everyone drank coffee, even kids. I shook my head and went to the fridge. The orange juice carton was empty but still sitting in the fridge. That would have prompted a lecture from M. The milk carton stood beside the coffee maker and had just enough to add to a couple more cups of coffee or a glass for me. I left it sitting there and filled a glass with water.

"Want me to make scrambled eggs?" I asked Paige.

"Please." Paige dropped onto a stool at the counter that served as both extra kitchen space and the only dining surface in the apartment.

Aunt Nell appeared in the living room just as I was dishing out the eggs onto three plates. She'd showered but still looked a bit like she was asleep as she shuffled around the corner toward us. Her foot caught the edge of my duffle bag that I kept tucked away beside the sofa. She stumbled for two steps until she righted herself and laughed at her clumsiness.

Some of my things spilled out of the open duffle. I went to put everything back, but she'd already stopped and started straightening it again. Her hand grasped the birthday card from M and Briony and was putting it back when she looked at it.

Her eyes widened as they shot up to meet mine. "Your birthday? When?" Her face scrunched up. "Oh, crap, last week. Oh, Livy, I'm so sorry. I can't believe I forgot."

"It's okay," I said because she looked pretty upset. It wasn't okay, but there was no point making her feel worse about it.

She came up to me and wrapped me in her arms. Paige joined in and patted my back. They shared a guilty look that they thought I couldn't read. "We'll get some cupcakes and candles today, okay? Twelve candles, right? You'll need two cupcakes to hold all those candles."

"Maybe three," Paige said in a cheery voice.

That was nice of them. A little late and not at all like the birthday plans I had, but still really nice of them. My aunt was trying and she seemed to be getting the hang of this parenting thing. I just had to give her more time. She loved me. I knew that. She made that clear. She just hadn't gotten to the point where she thought of me whenever she was making plans. That would come in time.

29

Closing a door never felt as good as it did just now. We'd barely been home from Boston before Caroline, Sam, Kayin, and Isabel insisted they come over for a game night. I absolutely hated hosting people at my house, but this was one of those things I had to get over when I married Briony. I couldn't ask her to keep her friends away, not when they used to come to her house for dinner or games or whatever. We'd had a reprieve for a year and a half when Caroline and Sam were caught up in having a baby and Kayin and Isabel were separated. These four had been tight with Briony from the beginning, but even she had gotten sick of some of their drama. Still, she tried to maintain a relationship with them even if they focused on their own lives to the point of not really carrying about anyone else. I honestly couldn't see what they had in common, but Briony liked a lot of variety in friends.

"Damn, I'm glad they didn't bring that baby." Briony leaned her forehead against the door I'd just closed behind "our" friends. "That makes me a bitch, but I really don't care."

I stroked her shoulder, completely agreeing but not needing to say it. It might make one of the few disagreements we had flare up again. I'd much rather go out to dinner with that group than have them over, but they all rotated houses for game night or movie night and Briony had always been in the rotation. When she first told me about it, I told her that wasn't going to happen. Flat out, didn't want any of them coming to our home. I'd never let anyone into my home other than a building manager and Briony. The idea of them coming here and passing judgment or seeing how I lived didn't sit well with me. Briony didn't appreciate my firm veto. She understood it at first, but the understanding waned the longer we lived together. She didn't want to become the social hermit I'd been and expected me to understand that and accommodate. My compromise was to take them out to dinner or a movie, but they didn't agree, so my only option was to accept it. I didn't like it, but Briony enjoyed it from time to time. At other times, she would have liked to use me as an excuse for begging off her turn in the rotation.

"Did you hate it?" Briony turned to face me.

I shrugged. She knew that I liked Isabel and Sam well enough. Kayin was more difficult for me because she asked direct and sometimes probing questions that I was never comfortable answering and made comments that made me feel inferior at times. Caroline now only talked about the baby. I was never a fan of babies.

"Once every three months, darling. Suck it up." She winked, knowing I'd lost this argument years ago.

"You're so understanding." I pinched her side and managed to slip past her revenge seeking hands on my way back to the living room. Several trips into the kitchen later, I had the living room as neat as I'd made it before the foursome descended.

"You tired?"

I was, exhausted actually. Briony didn't know just how much evenings like this took every ounce of energy I had. She believed I'd pushed through my anxieties to the point that I could at least stand to be in a room with the friends and partially enjoy myself. She didn't know that most of my evening was an act. She'd always place a hand on my back or thigh to help me calm when the panic started tightening and tightening until it felt like I couldn't breathe, but she didn't know how often that occurred with these friends. I couldn't tell her or she'd probably put an end to these evenings. Then she'd grow to resent me for it.

The phone rang before I could tell her I was tired enough to go to bed two hours early. I went to the kitchen to answer it.

"Is this Briony?" an unfamiliar voice asked.

"No, may I ask who's calling?"

"M? That's fine, I just, I," she sighed and rustling sounded as if she switched the phone to her other ear. "I forgot her birthday. I just, I forgot!"

With the added context, I finally figured out who was calling and my heart sank at her words. "Nell? Let me put you on speaker with Briony." I carried the receiver over to the couch and sat next to Briony. She wore a confused look as I pressed the speaker button. "Is everything okay? Is Olivia okay?"

"She's fine," Nell said in a small voice. "I just can't believe I missed her birthday. Her birthday!"

I widened my eyes at Briony. Poor Olivia. She'd been looking forward to us taking her to get her ears pierced because that's what her mom had wanted to do with her when she turned twelve. I wasn't even sure Olivia really wanted pierced ears, but her mother had decided she could get them pierced when she turned twelve, so that had been the plan.

"We're all human, Nell," Briony consoled her. "You've got a lot on your mind, and your situation is still new."

"I ruined her birthday. When I turned twelve, my sister and parents made a huge deal out of it. I invited my entire class out to a party. Olivia didn't get anything like that."

I wondered why she was telling us this. She certainly hadn't admitted to any failures when we spoke with her before. She didn't want to appear vulnerable at all. She'd shut down our hopes and now after she'd screwed up, she was seeking, what? Forgiveness? I wasn't feeling that magnanimous, but again, Briony's practice as a parent helped. She had dealt with many parents that she didn't agree with or like but still had to maintain politeness in order for Caleb to thrive.

"I'm sure Olivia understands," Briony assured her. I knew that was true, but it didn't make it right.

"You didn't forget. I saw the card you sent her. That's how I remembered."

No, we hadn't because we loved her as much as we loved Caleb, and you don't forget your kid's birthday.

"She didn't sound disappointed when we spoke to her." Briony tried to ease Nell's guilt.

"Oh, God, you called her, too? I'm the worst aunt ever."

I tried not to immediately agree. Olivia's twelfth birthday was supposed to solidify her role in our lives. We'd hoped to have the adoption in the works and planned to make her day as special as her mother would have made it. Treat her exactly as we had Caleb for his birthday celebration. She would not have questioned anything about how important she was to us after that day. But we never got to do that.

"It's going to be all right. Olivia knows you're doing everything you can for her. She's only going to remember that you were there for her to protect her and wish for her happiness."

"This comes so easily to you," she whispered with tears clogging her voice. She didn't sound resentful, just resigned.

"I have a lot more time doing this under my belt. I struggled in the beginning, too," Briony told her, but I didn't buy it. I wasn't sure Nell would either.

"I don't know," Nell admitted. "Maybe you guys were right. Maybe I need to think about things."

My heart started pumping because it sounded like Nell doubted herself and her ability to parent. Was she going back on her decision? It had only been two weeks since she'd shut us down.

"I don't even know where to start," Nell broke off with a sigh. "Maybe I should take a parenting class."

My eyes sought out Briony's. She'd looked hopeful for a moment, too. Parenting classes weren't what we wanted to hear.

"We're here for both of you," Briony said. "We want what's best for her. It's all we've wanted since meeting your niece."

"Thanks," Nell's voice turned resigned.

"Why don't we talk again tomorrow?" Briony suggested. "Today's been one of those hard parenting days. Tomorrow might be easier."

Damn good suggestion. I wish I'd thought of that. We'd surprised her when we told her about our adoption wishes. She reacted like any proud person who'd been taken by surprise. Now that she'd disappointed her niece and felt the shame in that, she might be more accepting of our desire to be a permanent part of Olivia's life.

Briony got her okay that we'd talk again tomorrow. She leaned her back against me and let out a long breath. Neither of us voiced what we were hoping this call would commence. Perhaps we were afraid to jinx it. But having Olivia's aunt reach out to us when she'd messed up with her meant she was beginning to trust our judgment as far as her niece was concerned. That could only lead to better things.

30

Olivia

Something big was going on. Nell and Paige had stayed up late talking, but I couldn't overhear what they were saying. I was starting to get worried about not being registered for school yet. I didn't want to bug them about it, but I knew I couldn't put it off much longer. I wouldn't get any good classes or be in the right locker area if we didn't get registered soon.

When I finished making breakfast, I sat and ate it alone because Paige and Nell hadn't woken up yet. I wondered if they had any more apartments for us to look at today. It seemed like we'd seen every building in town already. If not, Aunt Nell would probably just sit out on the balcony and listen to music with Paige for most of the day. I could borrow Paige's computer to look up nearby schools and walk over to see them. That would be one less thing for my aunt to deal with.

"Hey, Livy." Paige came into the kitchen with her hair tied back and her face scrubbed free of makeup.

"Hi, Paige. I made pancakes if you're hungry."

"You're handy to have around." Paige grinned and took a seat at the breakfast bar.

"Good morning." Aunt Nell joined us just after I'd slid a plate of pancakes on the counter. Her hair was still wet from a shower. Neither of them would be ready to go apartment hunting for another hour or two at the earliest.

I set her breakfast in front of her. Paige reached over to fill their coffee mugs. I sat back down and stared at my empty plate. I wanted to get up and wash it, but it would be rude to leave the counter before they even started eating. At Briony and M's we all ate together and no one left the table until everyone was done. I liked that rule.

They slowly finished breakfast. I tried to stop myself from asking what we were doing today. That question always bothered some of my foster families. They said it was too much pressure to plan my day. So I waited until they'd had their coffee and food before asking anything.

"Paige, could I borrow your computer this morning? I should look up some schools and maybe go check them out if we're not doing anything else."

Aunt Nell shot her a look before answering, "Why don't we hold off on that for today? We're expecting company around noon."

I waited for her to say more. She looked at Paige, who seemed to be trying to tell her something but wasn't doing a good job. They'd been doing this more and more lately. It was getting weird.

My aunt let out a long breath before she continued, "Your, um, that Briony and M are coming by."

My stomach did a backflip, but I tried not to look too excited to see them. It hurt Aunt Nell's feelings last time. I couldn't believe they were visiting today. I hoped they were going to ask me to do something with them again. Aunt Nell might let me this time now that she'd met them. I could go look for schools on Monday when everyone was at work.

I looked down at the hole in my jeans. I'd change to my other pair but they had a tear. Aunt Nell had gone to the store by herself last week, so I still hadn't gotten a sewing kit. Briony and M wouldn't say anything about it, but I wanted to look like I was doing okay here. Maybe my shorts would look best.

"Do you want me to make sandwiches?" I asked to take my mind off my clothes.

"I'm sure they'll have eaten by the time they get here."

"Is Caleb coming, too?"

"They didn't say." She clammed back up. She must know more, but she wasn't saying anything else.

I didn't want to bombard her with questions when she obviously didn't want to talk about it, but I had to ask, "If they ask me to go somewhere today, could I go?"

Aunt Nell thought for a moment. "You like them a lot, don't you?"

"Yeah, a lot. They were super nice to me."

"You liked living there?"

She'd never asked me that before. She'd asked about my other foster homes, but she hadn't asked me about Briony and M. The only time we really talked about them was after the lunch we shared together. I answered honestly even if Aunt Nell didn't like hearing it, "Yeah, I really liked it."

She studied me again for a while. Then she stood up and headed toward her bedroom. "We'll see when they get here."

That was almost a yes.

31

Olivia Briony and M seemed even happier to see me this time. We chatted for a long time about Caleb and his cousins and what they'd done in Vermont. Caleb was staying another week then he'd be coming back for school.

When they'd said everything about Vermont, there was this long pause. No one seemed to know what to say. Briony was never this uneasy, and Aunt Nell looked uncomfortable. Too bad Paige hadn't stuck around. She always made Aunt Nell feel more relaxed.

"Olivia," Briony finally began. "Your Aunt Nell, M, and I would like to talk about something with you."

They had something they all wanted to say to me? Maybe they wanted me to stay with them for the whole weekend. That would be great.

"We've missed you so much, Livy. The house just hasn't been the same without you. We knew you'd be in good hands with your aunt, but we've really missed you."

"Everyone else, too," M added.

Briony smiled and leaned forward to grasp my arm. "Before you came to live with your aunt, we were thinking how much we would have liked to have you stay with us."

"Like for another school year?" I sounded more hopeful than I should have since it didn't matter anymore. It did feel good that they might have wanted me for another year.

"Something like that," M said with a laugh.

"Would you have been okay with that?" Briony asked.

"Sure, yeah." I looked at my aunt and thought better of my answer. I didn't want to hurt her feelings. "I mean if Aunt Nell hadn't come for me."

Aunt Nell smiled but shot a look at Briony that I didn't understand.

"Of course. I know you've missed her. It's wonderful to have your aunt back." Briony released my arm to place her hand in M's. They did that more than they realized. Caleb would tease them about it, and they'd look surprised when he pointed out that they were holding hands. "We were hoping that you might want both."

"Both?"

"Be part of our family and have your aunt, too."

I was confused but didn't want to tell them that I couldn't figure out what they meant. "Like maybe you'll visit more?"

M shifted and faced me. "We told you before you came to live with your aunt that we'd love to have you stay with us. Remember? That hasn't changed. We still want you to live with us, but we also want you to have access to your aunt."

I'd live with them? How was that possible? I felt giddy as my heart started to pound. Then I glanced at my aunt. She looked like she might get sick. I really wanted to live with Briony and M, but that might make Aunt Nell really sad.

"Your aunt can visit anytime. She's always welcome at our home, and you could call her or text her whenever you want."

Aunt Nell gave Briony a surprised look. When she turned back to me, she didn't look as sad. "Would you want to do that, Livy?"

"Call and text you?" I asked, still not sure I was understanding this.

"Live with them but have visits with me and stay in constant contact?"

Could she really be saying this? "Is that okay with you?" I crossed my fingers that it was.

Her eyes welled up. "I want the best for you. I couldn't take you before when Nina died, and now that you've been here, I don't know if it's the best thing for you anymore. I know you liked living with them."

I did, so much, and I wanted to live with them again. "If it's okay with you, Aunt Nell, it's okay with me." I watched a tear race down her cheek. "If it makes you sad, I'll do whatever you want."

"Oh, God." Aunt Nell started crying. I didn't know what to do, but Briony did. She always did. She reached over and rubbed her back.

"You're not choosing between us," M spoke up. "You would live with us and have your aunt be your aunt. She would always be in your life. And you'd always be in our life. We're talking about adoption, not just fostering. Do you understand the difference?"

I think I did, but the girls at the group home said nobody my age gets adopted. So how could this happen? I asked what I hoped it meant, "Forever?"

M nodded and gave me one of those smiles that always made me feel so good. "Yes, that's the difference.

You'd never have to go to another foster home. Our house would be yours as much as it's Caleb's and ours. Your aunt is someone you can visit and talk to and love all you want, but you'll be part of our family, too."

Briony added, "We'd be your parents, Olivia. Not foster parents or people you're staying with. You'd be our daughter, and we'd be part of your life forever. We know you have a mom. We'll honor her always, but we want to be your moms, too." She held up three fingers. "You'd have three moms and an aunt and a brother and grandparents and cousins. We want that so much."

I looked back at Aunt Nell and saw that she'd stopped crying. She was looking at me with interest. Like she was waiting for me to decide. "Could I?"

"I've always wanted to be your aunt, Livy. Always. I want you in a place where you're happy and comfortable. Briony and M do that for you, don't they?"

I began to nod and kept nodding like I turned into a bobble head. My heart kept racing to where I felt a little dizzy. "Yeah, they do."

"Are you okay with one last move?" M asked me. Her eyes sparkled and her smile brightened the whole room.

"Back to your house?"

"Back to *our* house, yes." She waved her hand between us. "Whenever your aunt can visit, you can show off your room."

"Would you, Aunt Nell?" I bounced on the edge of the couch. "It's a super cool room. I chose the color, and we painted, and I have posters up, and my own desk. You could meet my friends, too."

She nodded and smiled. She slipped her arms around me for a long time. I couldn't believe this was happening.

"When?" I asked M.

"The adoption is going to take a while, but we'll file for temporary guardianship right away. Lauren is going to request an expedited hearing for this week because school starts the Tuesday after next. Does that sound okay with you?" She looked at both Aunt Nell and me.

I nodded that it sounded better than okay with me and jumped up to rush M. She caught me in a hug that made her lose the breath she was holding. She squeezed me just right but let me loose when Briony made a joyous sound and grabbed for me. Everything I'd wished for was given to me all at once.

32

Olivia For a second when I blinked awake, I couldn't remember where I was. I thought I'd dreamed the last week. Then I blinked again and purple surrounded me. So did my posters and my corkboard with pictures of my mom, Briony and M, Caleb and Hank, Eden and me, and the newest, Aunt Nell and me. I was home. My wishes had come true.

A soft knock on my door sounded before M poked her head inside. "Good morning, sunshine. First day of school. You up?"

I stretched and smiled. I used to hate the first day of school, but I felt like I might never hate anything again. "Yep."

"Up, up? Or am I coming back here in five minutes with a bucket of water?"

I giggled. M used humor to get us going. Briony would pounce and tickle. I didn't care whose turn it was to wake us up; I was just glad I got to experience it again. I pushed my covers back and sat up.

"Bri's making waffles."

"On a school day?" I tried not to sound shocked, but we usually just had cereal on weekday mornings.

"First day of middle school, Liv. Big day," M reported and went to knock on Caleb's door.

I jumped in the shower first. When I got out, M was still talking Caleb out of bed. He really didn't like waking up. I went into my room and opened the closet door. All my new clothes hung neatly on hangers. Clothes my aunt and Briony helped me pick out on two shopping trips while we were waiting for the guardianship to go through. Briony knew how to win my aunt over. Shopping. My aunt didn't care if it was for her or for me, so Briony used the excuse of school shopping when Aunt Nell got home from work two nights in a row. I shouldn't have let Briony and M spend so much money on a new school wardrobe, but it felt great to see my aunt and Briony with their heads together about the clothes I might like. Then later, Paige and Aunt Nell would root through the purchases to put together all the combinations of outfits for me. I couldn't remember what they chose for today.

"Know what you're wearing today?" M asked as she saw me standing in front of the closet still in my robe.

"I think so."

"Wear what makes you comfortable. You can try everyone else's suggestions once you've got your routine down at school."

I looked at her understanding eyes and wondered if she was reading my mind. Aunt Nell and Paige picked out something pretty for today. Briony picked a different shirt. Eden thought I should wear shorts and a t-shirt. I selected the short sleeve button up shirt that Briony liked and a pair of blue and white striped crop pants. Halfway between pretty and laidback.

Caleb opened the inner door of the bathroom as I clicked off the hairdryer. He was already dressed in new cargo shorts and a t-shirt with the logo of Quinn's basketball camp. He'd probably be bragging to all his friends that he'd gotten to work there this summer.

"Hey, Livy," He sounded more like a human than the grunting zombie who stumbled past me to shower minutes ago.

"Hi," I repeated my earlier greeting he must have missed.

"You nervous?"

Every possible emotion someone can have had already hit me all week long while we waited for the judge to sign the papers. I really didn't have time to dwell on how I should feel about starting at a new school today.

"Don't worry. I'll show you the trick to opening your locker in a hurry and let you in on all the shortcuts around school. I had your homeroom teacher last year. She's great. You'll like her."

"Okay, thanks." She could be the worst teacher ever, and I wouldn't care because I was home. I stowed the hairdryer under the counter and shared M's news, "They're making waffles."

His eyes brightened. They weren't quite as gold as Briony's but very near. "Mom always feels guilty on the first day of school. We can ask for anything this morning and she'll give it."

I laughed but knew that wasn't true. He'd already tried to get Briony to let us keep the cellphone that Willa had given me. I didn't care that she was taking it away until I started high school, but Caleb tried to come up with any way we could keep it to share. Not even guilt would make her change her decision on that one.

"Time?" he asked as he shoved a comb through his short hair.

I leaned out the door and looked into his room. The large red digital display said 00:22:13 then 00:22:12 and counting. I reported the time and headed for the stairs.

"Morning, sweetie. Ready for your first day?" Briony came over to my stool and kissed my forehead then squeezed an arm around me.

"Sure," I said, not feeling any of the apprehension I usually felt when I started a new school. It wouldn't be totally new, and all that mattered was that I'd be dropped off by M and picked up by Briony and tonight we'd be right back home.

After scarfing down on two waffles, I ran up to my room to grab my shoes and backpack. I checked that the new notebooks, pens, and calculator were inside before going back to the kitchen for the packed lunch M made.

Briony walked us to the door with lots of encouraging words. She pulled Caleb into a hug. "Have a good day, honey. I love you."

"Me, too, Mom," Caleb replied, patting her back twice before lurching toward the door. He was ready to see all his buddies again.

Her bright eyes accompanied a happy smile when I stepped up for my turn in the assembly line of hugs. "You have a good day, too, sweetie. I love you." She squeezed me tight.

"Thanks, Briony. Love you." I no longer held in those words around them anymore. They were going to be my parents. They wanted me. They loved me, and nothing felt better.

M kissed Briony and hustled us into her car. First stop was Hank's. His grandmother waved from her open door and wished us all a good first day. Then we drove to Eden's. I was really glad we were giving her a ride today because I didn't want to walk into school alone. Caleb and Hank might see some of their friends and ditch me, but Eden wouldn't.

"Morning," Eden's dad greeted us as we pulled into his driveway.

Eden's middle brother was getting into the beat up Jeep their oldest brother drove last year. The youngest brother raced out of the house and playfully shoved Eden on his way by. She stuck her foot out but was too slow to trip him. I wondered if I'd ever treat Caleb like the nuisance she thought her brothers were.

"Ah, so much love you have, sons," Eden's dad kidded them. "Don't bother saying goodbye like normal people or anything. Wouldn't want to wish your sister good luck on her first day of middle school and be mistaken for loving brothers."

If the oldest brother wasn't off at college this year, he might have had something really nice to say. Instead, the youngest brother scoffed and made a funny face with his fingers pulling at his lips and stuck his tongue out. Middle brother waved and called out from the driver's seat, "Don't do anything dorky on your first day, Eden. It'll stay with you all year."

Eden cupped her hand to her ear like she couldn't hear them. They did this a lot, but unlike other siblings I'd seen, they all actually liked each other. Eden waited until they screeched away in their car before giving her dad a hug and climbing into the backseat with me and Hank. She was in new shorts and a new t-shirt with a fancy design that her mom got her. Her hair grew about an inch over the summer, and it looked styled, a little like M's, which made me smile. It hadn't been styled yesterday when we spent the day at Willa's pool. I wondered if her middle brother, who was the king of hair product, had given her a lesson last night.

"Be good, kids." Her dad tapped the roof twice and M pulled away.

We barely had the chance to talk before we were at the middle school. Nerves hit me then, but one look at Eden and Caleb and the nerves left me. I had a best friend and a brother to be with this year. Nothing to be nervous about.

M parked and got out of the car with us. She reached out to grip my shoulder as the boys signed goodbye and started for the doors. "It's a whole new year," she whispered to me as she leaned in for a quick hug. "You'll do great. I couldn't be any more proud of you."

"Love you, M." I squeezed her tight before stepping back.

She pressed a hand to her heart then pushed us into motion with an encouraging smile. "Bye, girls. Have fun."

"What's your locker number?" Eden asked as we hurried to catch up with the boys. I pulled the paper from my backpack and told her. "Hope we're in the same area."

"Our lockers are over there," Caleb pointed down the first hallway inside the building. "Seventh grade lockers are this way."

"Cut through the commons to get to PE then use the locker room's outside exit to get over to your next class. It'll be faster," Hank told Eden when he looked over her schedule.

"You guys have PE together?" Caleb grabbed my schedule from my hands. "Good, but your next class is math, so that's back through the commons shortcut.

Homeroom and your first two classes are in the same hallway."

At our lockers, Eden and I high-fived when we saw that I was on one side of the U bank of lockers and she was on the other. It would make it easy to hang out between classes. Caleb showed us his trick with the lock then a group of his friends wandered by and pulled the boys away.

Eden slid down to sit on the floor in front of her locker. She patted the spot next to her. I sank down next to her as three girls that weren't from our elementary school did the same in front of their lockers. They smiled nervously and said hi. A boy I recognized had the locker next to Eden's. He glanced down at us as he banged on the door when it wouldn't open. Eden popped up and showed him Caleb's trick to get his locker open. She was just sitting back down when Krystal and Kortney walked by. Their last names should put them in the other bank of lockers, but that didn't keep them from stopping.

"Lookey here, Kortney. The freak twins are together again." She smirked at Kortney and signaled for the rest of her pack to surround us. To Eden she said, "Still can't decide if you're a girl or a boy?" Then she turned her sneer to me. "Surprised you passed the sixth grade, dumbbell."

The guy next to Eden slammed his locker and faced Krystal. "Grow up."

Eden and I shared a surprised look at his words and watched as he pushed past Krystal's group. The girls sitting near us frowned and shook their heads. They probably had their own set of mean girls to look out for.

"Did you forget how to talk over the summer?" Krystal taunted me. "Maybe you should be in the special school."

Eden spoke up as she usually did whenever Krystal got on a roll. "It's great that you put on some weight this summer, Krystal. You looked like a stick figure last year."

The girl pack gasped at Eden's suggestion that Krystal got heavy over the summer. If she had, it would have been a mean thing to say. But the only extra padding she had this year was in her bra.

"Shut up, freak," Krystal screeched at her.

"Hey, Liv," Caleb called out from behind the pack. They parted to look at him and, as one, started twirling the ends of their hair and smiling stupidly. "Ready to walk to your homeroom?" His eyes passed over every girl, lingering on Krystal with a look I'd never seen on him before. He got along with everyone, liked everyone, but this look didn't say he liked her.

"Hi," she almost sang out to him. I knew that tone. She thought he was cute. "I'm Krystal."

Caleb looked at her again. "I'm Olivia's brother."

Her eyes practically fell out of her head as she looked at him then at me and back to him. "He's your brother? I thought Mrs. Lomax said you didn't have a family."

Eden and I got to our feet. Caleb came to stand beside me. He looked like he was going to stick up for me again, but something swelled in my chest. Something powerful like I've never felt before. I met her stare and announced, "I have one now."

"With an awesome brother," Caleb inserted and flashed me a cocky smile. "And buddies who'll always be close by." His hand gestured to Hank, Terrance, and several of his other friends all waiting to walk with us.

His meaning was clear. Krystal would have a hard time talking about Eden and me the way she had last year without one of Caleb's friends hearing about it. Her brand of mean fun just got cut off, and my seventh grade existence just hurtled past the best of any other grade.

33

Waiting in the lobby of Jessie's gym always provided entertainment. Members came and went. Everyone seemed to know each other because Jessie fostered a community atmosphere. Rare was the person who just walked through the lobby and over to the security gate on a mission to get to her workout. I could spend hours watching the people here. I never minded that Willa took five minutes longer to dry her hair after our workouts together.

"Hey, M," Jessie called out as she sailed down the stairs from her office. "How's things?"

I smiled at her as she greeted a few other people who were grabbing beverages from the juice bar. I expected her to continue on to whatever class she was teaching based on her exercise ready appearance, but instead she stopped in front of me.

"Good, thanks. You?" I glanced up and up some more at Jessie's six foot one inch frame. "Willa said the expansion is going to be done before winter?"

She nodded and smiled with what looked like pride. "Sure is. We were lucky to get the space next door. Des had fun knocking through walls for a while. You like racquetball?"

I shrugged, not really one way or another on the sport. Willa was jazzed about the courts going in, so I knew we'd be spending at least one of our workout mornings playing as soon as they were done.

"Willa's orders."

I wondered if that was really the only reason her expansion included two racquetball courts. I wouldn't put it past Jessie. She was pretty damn good at being a friend.

"How're my favorite kids?"

My smile this time was pretty wide. Kids, plural. Nothing felt better. Olivia was back and everything was right in our world. Thanks to Lauren's efficient work getting the papers filed, the home study would be completed in a few weeks, a month at the most. "They're good. Olivia is loving soccer and Caleb's trying his legs at cross-country this year."

Her head tilted back with even more pride because she knew she was the influence behind Caleb's interest in running. Nothing like an Olympic bronze medalist in the heptathlon to inspire a young man's mind. Especially when he worshipped her to begin with. "When are the next events? I called Bri about it, but she couldn't find the schedule when we talked."

I tried not to let my surprise show. "You want to go?"

"Sure. It's no secret we like your kids." She leaned down with a teasing smile and looked like she might bump my shoulder. I almost took a step back but didn't need to because this was Jessie. Once when she'd been my personal trainer, she tried to correct my form by placing her hands on my shoulder and side. I flinched so hard she jumped back a foot. She never tried touching me again.

"Saturday morning for soccer and Caleb's running Tuesday night. I'll text you the times and places." The kids would be thrilled to see Jessie at their activities. I was again amazed by how good a friend she could be when most of the friends gave her a hard time for being casual about so many things.

A minute after Jessie left to teach her spinning class, Willa showed up. A gym bag dangled from one elbow as she finished slipping her other arm through a light blazer. "Ready?"

We'd just spent an hour on various weight machines. It used to be free weights, but we'd have to spot each other. Now we preferred the machines so we could work out together and not worry about adding and subtracting weights along the way.

I nodded and fell into step with her. "Do you have time for coffee before work?"

She glanced at me as we exited. Her eyes shot back to the door. She was probably wondering why I waited until we'd left before proposing coffee. We could have gotten it at the little stand inside. "Sure, Caroline's?"

"Uh," I hesitated and thought about how busy Caroline's deli would be right now. "Someplace a little quieter."

She came to a full stop and turned. Her brown eyes swept over me briefly before nodding. "Want to grab a coffee and head back to my house?" She read my mind and added, "Quinn's off to work already."

"Your place, yes."

We got into my car, stopped at a drive thru coffee place, and made the short drive back to her house where I'd picked her up earlier. She chatted about Quinn's best recruit this year, somehow knowing I wasn't ready to start the conversation I'd asked for.

When she let us inside, she followed me toward her living room. "Please say you're not moving?"

I pushed out a relieved breath. "Not moving."

"Oh, good." She turned and dropped onto the sofa with a sigh. "You had me scared there."

Her words warmed my heart. She was such a good friend to me. From the moment we met at her office when I brought my first operations class to see how her company worked, through the years of hanging out with just each other, to being forced to become part of her group when I met Briony, Willa had been the best friend I'd ever had. That she'd be upset if I moved was a wonderful and very welcome thing.

She took a sip of her latte and waited me out. She almost never rushed me.

"As long as nothing goes wrong with the home study, Olivia's adoption could finalize in a few months, maybe sooner."

She nodded like I hadn't already told her this. When I didn't offer more, she encouraged, "That's great."

"Yeah." Amazing and more than I could have hoped for in my life. "She's taking my name."

Willa popped forward in her seat. "M, that's great. Really great. I thought with her birth mom and everything that she'd want to keep her last name."

"Me, too, but I guess her mom wasn't too fond of the name to begin with and with her grandparents being..."

"Pig-headed dicks?" Willa guessed with a smirk.

"Pretty much, so I guess that was part of it, but she really wants to be part of the family."

A frown creased her forehead. "But Caleb has Briony's name."

"She thinks it'll combine us all even more."

"She's smart, that one."

"She's the best."

"Olivia Desiderius," she mused. A smile appeared as her thumb tapped her chin twice. "Sounds just right. Congratulations, M. I said it before, but you've done a wonderful thing here, and it's all the better because she's just as wonderful."

I tucked my chin against my chest. "Anyway, that will make her officially ours and with that…" I tried to piece together what I wanted to say. I'd rehearsed it, but it wasn't coming out smoothly. I should have let Briony come with me, but I thought it might add too much pressure on Willa. I needed her to give me an honest answer not a pressured one. "I wanted to ask you…"

"Yes?" She sat forward, her eyes earnest.

"This is harder than I thought."

"Whatever it is, I'll do it."

I tried to keep from scoffing in disbelief. "You can't know that."

"What did I tell you about personal favors for friends?"

That she'd always do them. "But this is more than just a favor."

"I know you'd never ask me for something I can't or won't give. I'd never do that you to either."

"This is," I didn't finish. I needed to shut up and stop convincing her that she'll decline. "Since Olivia will be ours legally, I don't want her to worry about…that is, Briony says her parents would, but if Caleb is with one of his aunts and Briony's parents are older, and Olivia doesn't really know them yet, and what if it happened before she did?" Now I was just talking in circles. This wasn't any better.

"M?" she waited for me to focus on her. "That sounds like you're talking about guardianship. Are you asking me to be Olivia's guardian if something happens to you and Briony?"

"Yes, I am. We are," I corrected because Briony was worried, too. Caleb's guardianship was settled, but with Olivia barely knowing Briony's parents right now, we had to think what might work best for her. "Olivia's only met Briony's parents once. They'll be down for the adoption signing and we'll be back at Christmas, but if something happened to us before she really got to know them..." I looked up to catch Willa's understanding nod. "I want her to have a choice."

Willa pulled in on her bottom lip, a sign she was thinking. Nothing in her expression told me she wanted me to leave right now after making such an outrageous request.

"It's just, I can't allow for her not to have someone. I can't leave that up in the air. And please know that you don't have to agree. This is a major decision. I want her to have an option besides Briony's parents. I can't let her go through this ever again. I had to—" I cut myself off before I told her too much. I'd never told anyone but Briony about being in foster care. Willa might have guessed, especially since I didn't talk about what it was like for me growing up. Sure, she could have guessed, but I didn't feel comfortable talking about it.

"You don't want her to be relegated to foster care again. I don't either," she agreed quietly, looking off through the French doors to her pool deck. It was one of the reasons I was asking her to be Olivia's guardian rather than Briony's suggestion of Jessie. Sure, Jessie hung out with the kids, was basically a big playmate for

Caleb, and obviously adored them. But Willa loved the kids, Olivia specifically. I could see it in the way she talked to them. In the way she walked with them, always making sure she knew exactly where they were whenever we were out together. How it mattered what they were doing, if they were having fun, and if they were getting everything they needed to be happy.

"Just, if you could consider it, please. You obviously have to talk to Quinn, but consider it."

She let out a long breath. "I don't need to. I'd be honored to take care of her if the worst happened."

Just like that? This wasn't Briony I was talking to. Willa considered things. Took time. Didn't have kids for a reason. Then again, she knew exactly what she'd be getting with Olivia. Maybe it was that easy. It certainly had been for me. "That's...thank you, but I know you need to talk to Quinn."

"Do I?" she asked with a grin. "Would you have to ask Briony?"

Would I? No. If I wanted to take on the guardianship of another child, she wouldn't stop me. Should I? Yes, but again, it wouldn't be necessary. Briony was like that. Apparently Quinn was, too.

"M, you don't need to worry about Olivia. She will always have options and family. If you and Briony are sure about this, I'd like to meet her parents again. If something were to happen, we'd need to work together for Olivia's sake. She can stay temporarily or permanently, whatever she wants. She'll never be without a choice or a home again."

God, I wanted to hug her. I'd never wanted to hug anyone other than Briony and the kids, but now I wanted to hug my friend. My best friend, who listened to my greatest fear and made it go away. I felt tears push heavily against my eyes.

"If we did take over guardianship, don't worry on my end. If something happens before she's out on her own and Briony's parents aren't in a position to take her in, she'll have my sister or my mom, and as a last resort, my lame-ass brother, who's only a lame-ass as a brother, but a great father to my nephew."

I really wanted to hug her. This friend of mine. Everything I'd thought about, wanted to go through with her, for the security of Olivia's future, she just talked through.

"Thank you, Willa."

My hand reached out on its own. It was a full second before my brain caught up and yanked it back. The space between us seemed to stretch for miles but wasn't more than a few feet. I could do this. I should do this. It wasn't enough to just thank her. With both brain and hand working together, I reached out again. My fingers curled over the top of her hand, palm resting flat. The initial static shock pulsed through leaving a slight tingling in my fingers, but I forced my hand to remain gripping hers. I waited for the next sensation of pain, like badly scraped palms, but it never came. Amazing.

"M," Willa said softly and squeezed my hand in return. This was the first time I consciously touched my friend, and bless her; she didn't make a big deal about it.

"You're a good friend," I told her. "Always so good to me."

"Same here, the best, actually." She smiled.

I pulled my hand back, setting it on my thigh. "Talk to Quinn, even if you don't have to, please do. We'd like to have Lauren re-do our wills as soon as the adoption goes through."

"I will. Tonight. No need to worry. She adores Olivia as much as I do."

I stood and she did the same. The conversation went exactly as I'd hoped. Better than I thought it would. As amazing as my life had been over the last few years, I shouldn't be surprised when things worked out better than I expected anymore.

Epilogue

Two Months Later

M The alarm on my laptop beeped. I glanced at the clock, amazed that it was almost time for dinner. I had one more paper to grade, but I didn't care. Before I would have plowed through, would have worked until I'd forgotten to eat, until my eyes closed from exhaustion. I'd fallen asleep at my desk many nights before Briony came into my life. I didn't need to keep working. I would get the paper done tomorrow before my first class. I didn't let anything get in the way of spending time with Briony and the kids.

Shutting down the laptop, I stretched and popped out of the chair. I straightened up the desk in case Briony needed to get some work done later. When we moved into this place, we had two separate offices, but once Olivia came to live with us, we started sharing the den downstairs. I wasn't sure I could do that, but Briony mostly gets her work done in the living room and rarely needs to use the office when I need to.

I headed upstairs to check on the kids. Caleb was lounging on the loveseat in the bonus room at the top of the stairs. He was fidgeting and tapping his pencil on the pad of paper that sat on the coffee table. He had a desk in his room, but he usually liked to do his homework out here.

"I hate algebra!" he declared as soon as he saw me coming up the stairs. The petulance that had surfaced at times over the summer had vanished. Spending time with his grandparents and cousins had helped, but it was having our family whole again that really brought back the considerate boy I knew and loved. "Don't say I'm going to need this when I get older, M. I don't buy it."

I smiled. That was his mom's favorite saying when he pushed back on his homework. "Unfortunately, your mom's right on this one."

"Will there ever be anything I learn that I won't need?"

"Geography."

His eyes popped because I'd actually given him an answer. "Seriously?"

"It's nice to know countries and locations, but you'll find it changes over time. Europe has several more countries now than when I studied geography in school. So memorize all you like, but it'll change by the time you get to my age."

"Ancient?" he joked.

"Decaying," I confirmed. "Need help yet?"

He shook his head and sighed dramatically as he looked back at his book.

"Dinner will be ready soon," I reported and turned to head into Olivia's bedroom. She preferred to sit at her desk for homework unless she needed help, then she'd bring her books to the dining table. We had a rule that they needed to try to get their homework done on their own at first. "How's it going in here?"

Olivia looked up from her textbook and smiled. She had two rulers placed on the book to help keep her place when she read. It was a technique I'd done research on when Briony and I recognized some of Olivia's learning blocks. We hadn't had her tested for dyslexia yet because we wanted her to settle into this family unit with us. We knew she felt inadequate academically and didn't want to inflate that notion by making her take a test that would confirm a learning disability. In the seventh grade, it wouldn't make much difference to have it verified. We'd wait until next year before testing and seeking a specialized tutor.

"Almost done. Just two more pages," she said. "Did you know that Julius Caesar was stabbed twenty-three times by some of the senators he worked with?"

I walked up behind her and looked down at the world history text she was reading. "I'd heard that, yes. Did you know that we have Julius Caesar to thank for revising the calendar to follow the solar year, not the lunar cycle? And that the first of the year wasn't always January first?"

She turned in her chair to face me, eyes wide with wonder. This was one of the many things I loved about her. She really liked to learn. It was difficult for her, but she loved learning something new. If I told her everything she'd learn from reading that book, she'd retain it all. She was one of the best auditory learners I'd seen.

"When was it?" she asked.

"Their new year started in March not January." I reached out and pulled her ponytail free of the hoody she was wearing. "How many sides does an octagon have?"

Her eyes darted up before she responded, "Eight."

"That's right. So which month should October be?"

Her eyes flashed when she realized the answer. "Eighth."

"Very good. Now for the bonus round; which month do you think is named after Julius Caesar?"

She thought for a while before the answer came to her. "July!"

"You're so smart." I slipped that in during every homework session to reinforce what I knew to be true about her intelligence. She could doubt it from time to time, but my goal was to make her believe it always. "And just so you know, August is for Augustus Caesar. You'll probably read about him next."

"How do you know all this stuff?"

"Nerds know stuff."

She giggled and my heart warmed at the sound. She was more talkative and open and laughed a lot now. It was as if the second she knew she was here to stay, she felt safe to be herself. And I loved this secure, sweet girl.

"You're not a nerd, Mom."

I still drew in a breath every time she called me Mom. Briony had held a family meeting when we passed the home study and knew we'd be getting the best recommendation from the case worker. She expressed our hope that Olivia would start calling us Mom or whatever she felt comfortable with. It took a week before Olivia let it slip the first time. After that, when she was sure she'd be ours, Briony and I were Mom. Both of us, which I liked, even when we both responded if she called to us.

"Nothing wrong with being a nerd, sweetie. Both your moms are nerds, and we're going to do everything we can to turn you into one."

"Good luck with that." Caleb joined us at the open door. "We're too cool for that. You and Mom can be in your own nerd cult. Don't try to recruit us."

Caleb was developing his mom's sense of humor. He could make me laugh almost as much as his mom could. "Dinner's soon, kids."

"Does Mom need help?" Olivia asked because that was exactly like her.

"We'll handle it. Get your homework done so we can have a final showdown of badminton after dinner. The net comes down tonight before it's too cold to spend any time outside anymore."

They both yelped with excitement as I made my way downstairs. Briony was humming in the kitchen, the best sign that she was happy.

"Hi, hon," she greeted. "Did you get the papers graded?"

"All but one."

She turned and gave me a sly smile. "And you're not itching to get that done? Not feeling an unnatural pull back to the office to get that one little ol' paper done. An obsessive need to finish it?"

I couldn't help but laugh at her tease. She'd been working on my tendencies, which she called compulsions, to finish things before moving on to something else. After the honeymoon wore off, these compulsions of mine started to get under her skin. I worked on them so I could now walk away without finishing a task if something else needed tending. Dinner prep and stolen moments with Briony were worth abandoning whatever I was doing. But sometimes I liked driving her a little batty. It made up for the things she did that made me want to grind my teeth.

"What can I help with?"

"Pork chops are almost done. The stuffed zucchini should be pulled out of the oven. I'll have the kids put together the salad when they get down here."

"Tasty."

She smiled and leaned in for a quick kiss. "Yes, you are."

My stomach tingled at the look in her eyes. I slid my hands up her arms and pulled her closer. She dropped the spatula she was holding and wrapped her arms around my neck. In the next second my mouth was sliding against hers. Pliant, soft, tantalizing lips teased me before her tongue plucked at my lower lip twice and pushed inside to stroke mine. Kissing had become one of my favorite activities. Something I'd never done for thirty-six years dominated my to-do list every day now. I was lucky to find a partner that felt the same.

"Damn, woman, you're winding me up at the exact wrong time."

"Oh?" I teased, pushing her against the counter and lifting her legs.

She yelped in surprise and placed her hands on the counter to help me lift her into a seated position. "You are so bad."

"We have some time."

"We have no time, and you know it."

"I know, but I like winding you up. You'll be on fire by the time the kids hit the sack tonight."

She leaned down to kiss me again. Her fingers stroked down my chest, brushing over one breast before gliding back up. "We'll starve if we don't stop right now."

"I'm good with starving." My hands slid up her thighs and gripped her hips, pulling them against my stomach.

"Mom!" Caleb yelled as he thundered down the stairs.

I pulled back, both regret and promise in my eyes as I moved from between her legs. She slid off the counter with the same expression but started chuckling just as quickly. Life with kids meant constant interruptions.

"What's for dinner?" Caleb asked as he came in the kitchen. He eyed us with suspicion for a second. I resisted checking to see if my hair was mussed.

"You'll find out when you sit at the table. Get a salad started and call your sister to set the table."

"Livy!" he bellowed from the middle of the kitchen.

Briony shook her head and sighed. "I meant, go get her, don't yell from down here."

"Yeah, yeah," he muttered, racing out of the kitchen to the bottom of the stairs to yell again.

Briony turned to me. "I am speaking English, right?"

I laughed at her constant battle to get Caleb to follow instructions when he had a very stubborn mind of his own. I turned to pull the zucchini pan out of the oven when her hand stopped me. The look in her eyes added ten degrees to the room.

"Tonight, we're finishing what you tried to start here, sexy," she vowed and planted another kiss on me as the kids joined us. "Done with homework?"

"Done," they both said.

"How do your ears feel, sweetie?" Briony asked Olivia, her fingers going to trace the shell of Olivia's ear and touching the peridot stone that glittered there.

"These are so much better than those piercing studs, Mom," Olivia reported, her fingers flicking the other stone. "I love them."

"They're perfect for you, kiddo," I said, happy that she'd been able to get her ears pierced on the schedule her mom had planned for her. Briony had pulled off the perfect birthday celebration for Olivia, giving her the day she wanted with her friends and getting her ears pierced as promised. That almost as much as telling her we wanted to adopt her gave Olivia all the security she seemed to need. Even when her aunt came to visit a few weeks ago, Olivia didn't show any of the shyness or hesitation she'd shown when we'd seen them together the last time. She was thriving in our home and her aunt seemed both relieved and thrilled for her niece.

"Eden's trying to get permission to pierce hers now instead of next year like her dad promised," Olivia told us.

"Maybe I should get a piercing," Caleb said as he brought the salad bowl to the table.

"One from your top lip to your bottom lip with a nice big fastener?" Briony teased.

"Oh, funny. Mom's a comedian." He elbowed Olivia, happy to have a coconspirator in all things anti-parental now. "We'll go broke if she goes out on tour."

"Clever," Briony told him, handing him the pork serving dish and Olivia the zucchini. She turned back to me and slipped her arms around my waist, bringing her mouth to mine.

"Again with the kissing," Caleb declared in an exaggerated sigh. He rolled his eyes at Olivia this time, but she wasn't nearly as bothered as he was by our PDAs.

"How would you like it if I mocked you when you start kissing your girlfriends?" his mom taunted.

"M's not your girlfriend, Mom. You're married. You should be over the kissing by now."

We laughed. My hand went to Briony's back, rubbing a familiar pattern. She turned a breathtaking smile my way before telling him, "It doesn't work that way, bud. Get used to it."

He shook his head like he'd never understand his mom. I turned back to Briony and sighed happily. I could definitely get used to evenings just like this one for many years to come.

If you enjoyed *Forevermore*, don't miss the book that introduced M and Briony to the Virginia Clan, *Blessed Twice*. Read an excerpt on the following pages.

Blessed Twice

Briony There were about a million other things I could be doing right now. Playing tennis, reading a mystery, calling my son at summer camp, working out, rollerblading, base jumping, banging my head against a low hanging beam, and all would be more pleasant than my sixth first date. Cripes, my friend Caroline knew a lot of women. A lot of women who were so wrong for me.

This one's name was Polly, and she worked as a court clerk. After her third cup of coffee—I'd learned never to commit to anything that would last several courses—I could sum up Polly's personality with one word: drama. Or, issues. Or, get me the hell out of here, please!

"And then I was, like, 'what do you think you're doing with my stuff, bitch?' I mean, like, can you believe she was walking out on me and expected to take the one and only gift she, like, bought me in the entire two months we'd been together? I was, like, 'you didn't even pay me rent for two months, you're not taking my Maroon 5 with you.'" Her pretty green eyes stared expectantly at me, asking me to agree.

Still stuck on some of the other intimate details she'd shared prior to talking about a massive blowout over a piece of plastic that costs twelve dollars, I merely nodded then shook my head. I didn't know if she expected me to say, "Yes, I completely agree, even though you're a loon," or, "No, that's just awful, especially since there's no way you could ever replace such a priceless item. Unless, of course, you walked into any music store, or better yet, downloaded the songs so no one can walk out of your life with her love and your CDs."

"You're so easy to talk to," she jabbered on after I'd apparently given the appropriate response. "I can't believe Caroline never introduced us before. I'm having so much fun." Yeah, because drinking coffee is a riot a minute. "So, like, what's your story?"

Well, I've never used the word "like" as a verbal pause, I've never moved in with someone after one night together, and I've never considered a CD worth the effort of an argument. Oh, and I now deem dating a soul draining experience.

"Briony?"

I looked up and felt my stomach plunge as swiftly as if I'd been pushed out of an airplane. M was standing by my table, iced coffee in hand on her way out. She was in casual clothes, showing a hint of midriff, envious calves, and just the barest promise of cleavage. "Hey there, M." I hoped she caught the relief in my tone. Wow, she looked good. No makeup today and her hair was a little more chaotically styled but wickedly attractive. Beyond, actually, more like hot. Yes, hot suited her just fine. Why wasn't I on a date with her? Oh, crap, Polly. "This is Polly. Polly, my friend and colleague, M."

Polly must have picked up on my blatant interest in M, because the next thing I knew, she was telling her, "We'd invite you to join us, but we're on a date."

I didn't know who cringed more, me at the idea that this could really be counted as a date or M at the rude dismissal. My eyes snapped up to hers in apology. Before I realized what I was doing, I made the ASL sign for "help." It was one of a few words I'd learned for when my son spent time with his hearing impaired best friend. This was the first time I'd ever used it, and I never imagined I'd be using it for evil instead of good.

"Pardon the intrusion, but I thought we said two o'clock?" M asked me with the perfect amount of urgency and innocence. "I grabbed a table up front and left all the lecture notes and business plans there. It's a few hours of work, and I've got plans tonight, but if you need a little more time, I understand."

"Is it two o'clock already?" I brought my wrist up to check the time on my watch. "Gosh, I'm sorry, Polly. I didn't mention this work thing because I never thought we'd still be here. You just made the time fly by." Two hours that I'll never, ever get back.

She beamed at my compliment but disappointment showed through. "Caroline said you were a workaholic, but we can work on that." She reached for a hug, which I made lightning quick, and finally, the sixth date on my path through hell was over. Polly banged through the coffeehouse doors with all the drama she'd expressed during her diatribe.

"Thank you for saving me."

"Think nothing of it." M said it like she believed it when I was considering erecting a life-sized shrine and lighting a candle every night. Her eyes darted to the door as her customary introversion returned. "Nice running into you, Briony. Enjoy the rest of your weekend."

"Tell me about those plans you mentioned," I blurted before she could disappear.

"I lied," she admitted with a shy smile. "I figured if I didn't give a limited window of time, she might think she could get us to postpone our work meeting."

Strangely, I felt more relief hearing this than getting out of my date with Polly. "So you've got nothing going?" She shook her head. I smiled and stepped toward her. "You do now."

I couldn't think of a better way to spend my Saturday than with this beautiful, enticing woman. Not really a date, but far better than anything my friends could set up for me.

OTHER PUBLICATIONS BY LYNN GALLI

VIRGINIA CLAN

Wasted Heart (Book 1) – Attorney Austy Nunziata moves across the country to try to snap out of the cycle of pining for her married best friend. Despite knowing how pointless her feelings are, five months in the new city hasn't seemed to help. When she meets FBI agent, Elise Bridie, that task becomes a lot easier.

Imagining Reality (Book 2) – Changing a reputation can be the hardest thing anyone can do, even among her own friends. But Jessie Ximena has been making great strides over the past year to do just that. Will anyone, even her good friends, give her the benefit of the doubt when it comes to finding a forever love?

Blessed Twice (Book 3) – Briony Gatewood has considered herself a married woman for fifteen years even though she's spent the last three as a widow. Her friends have offered to help her get over the loss of her spouse with a series of blind dates, but only a quiet, enigmatic colleague can make Briony think about falling in love again.

Finally (Book 4) – Willa Lacey never thought acquiring five million in venture capital for her software startup would be easier than suppressing romantic feelings for a friend. Having never dealt with either situation, Willa finds herself torn between what she knows and what could be.

ASPEN FRIENDS

Mending Defects (Book 1) – Small town life for Glory Eiben has always been her ideal. With her rare congenital heart defect, keeping family and friends close by preserves her easygoing attitude. When Lena Coleridge moves in next door, life becomes anything but easy. Lena is a reluctant transplant and even more reluctant friend. Their growing friendship adds many layers to Glory's ideal.

Something So Grand (Book 2) – A designer for the wealthy, Vivian Yeats doesn't have time for relationships, yet she longs for romance. She's had to settle in the past when it comes to women but won't bother to again. If romance is going to happen for her, it'll take someone special to turn her head. Natalie Harper, the new contractor on her jobsites, might just be the woman to do it.

Life Rewired (Book 3) – Two years ago, Molly Sokol decided she wanted to get serious about finding that special someone. She could picture her perfectly—petite, feminine, excitable, adoring, and ultra-affectionate. When the opposite of all that comes along in the form of Falyn Shaw, Molly never thought they'd be anything more than friends. Being wrong has never felt so good.

OTHER ROMANCES

Uncommon Emotions – When someone spends her days ripping apart corporations, compartmentalization is key. Love doesn't factor in for Joslyn Simonini. Meeting Raven Malvolio ruins the harmony that Joslyn has always felt, introducing her to passion for the first time in her life. (Special Edition includes epilogue never before in print.)

Full Court Pressure – The pressure of being the first female basketball coach of a men's NCAA Division 1 team may pale in comparison to the pressure Graysen Viola feels in her unexpected love life.

About The Author

Lynn Galli resides in the Pacific Northwest where she enjoys long walks on rocky beaches in the rain and standing in everlasting lines for a complex cup of coffee that will sustain her on a fifty-five minute, ten mile drive to her job writing software programs that allow her to build airplanes, save wildlife, and promote recycling. Her chilly summer evenings are usually spent writing about places that are much warmer and drier but nowhere near as beautiful or bursting with coffee, airplane manufacturing, and software coding.

CPSIA information can be obtained at www.ICGtesting.com
Printed in the USA
BVOW05s1421220914

367818BV00001B/105/P